The Serial Sneak Thief

By the Same Author

The Purloined Corn Popper

(THE MCGURK MYSTERY SERIES)
The Case of the Wiggling Wig
The Case of the Absent Author
The Case of the Fantastic Footprints
The Case of the Desperate Drummer
The Case of the Weeping Witch

(OTHER BOOKS)
Hester Bidgood, Investigatrix of Evill Deedes
The Ghost Squad Breaks Through
Time Explorers, Inc.

A FELICITY SNELL MYSTERY

The Serial
Sneak Thief

E. W. HILDICK

MARSHALL CAVENDISH   NEW YORK

To Jessica and Jennifer Hutchinson,
in whose parents' holiday cottage, "Camellia,"
Felicity Snell, her adventures, and her background
first began to take shape.

Marshall Cavendish
99 White Plains Road
Tarrytown, New York 10591-9001

Library of Congress Cataloging-in-Publication Data
Hildick, E. W. (Edmund Wallace), date.
The serial sneak thief / by E.W. Hildick. — 1st ed.
        p.   cm.
Summary: A master criminal known as The Chameleon threatens to disrupt a mystery contest
being held in the public library, but J.G. and the other Watchdogs are on hand to investigate.
ISBN 0-7614-5011-4
[1. Contests—Fiction. 2. Libraries—Fiction. 3. Mystery and detective stories.] I. Title.
PZ7.H5463Ser   1997   [Fic]—dc21   97-8425   CIP   AC

The text of this book is set in 12 point Sabon
Printed in the United States of America
First Edition

1   3   5   6   4   2

Contents

The Serial Sneak Thief

A Contest Is Announced

Saturday, September 12, is a date that always brings a cloud to Felicity Snell's face whenever she thinks of it. Not that she thinks of it for more than a minute or two. Nothing gets her down for long. But the events of that day nearly did.

They came so close to ending her career as Children's Librarian in disaster and disgrace.

Both her careers, in fact. Because, at one point, it didn't look like they were doing much good for her reputation as a crack private detective, either!

The day itself started out peacefully enough. The sky above the Ebenezer Twitchpurse Memorial Library in West Milbury was a clear blue. The sun lit up the front of the ivy-shrouded building and actually made it seem inviting. The ivy leaves seemed to beckon as they were stirred by a light breeze, with the sunlight dancing and flickering on their dark green and red surfaces.

"Hey! Hold it! Wait!" they seemed to whisper. "Don't go away! Wait till you hear what's in store for you today! Wait till . . ."

And then, suddenly, with a loud clapping noise, a huge banner was unfurled between the peaks of the twin towers at either side of the building and the message spread its large black letters on white against the blue sky:

Cheers arose from the early arrivals down below on the sidewalk. This was followed by another cheer as a second banner was lowered from the battlements between the towers by the two men who'd set the first one flapping and fluttering overhead. This one read:

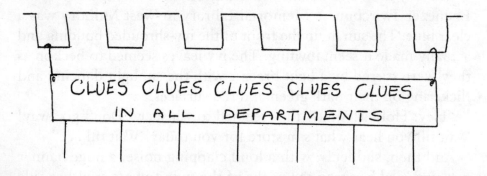

And as it was stretched out, a number of white squares tumbled out of it to hang suspended on strings at different levels—some swaying in front of the windows and others nestling in the ivy. Each card bore one simple message. A black question mark.

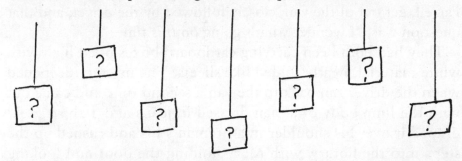

A murmur of recognition went through the crowd. They'd seen something like this before, downtown. Many times. And on a very similar building—Rubinstein's Department Store. It had twin towers also, with the same kind of battlements. It had been built around the same time—about 130 years ago—by the same architect.

The ivy had long since been removed from the Rubinstein building and the first floor had been remodeled with large, plate glass windows. But the rest of the building was just like the library. Especially this morning, with the banners. Several times a year, Rubinstein's blossomed with banners. Except, in their case, the sign up top usually proclaimed GREAT ONE-DAY WHITE SALE or GREAT ONE-DAY RED TAG SALE; the sign below boasted of BARGAINS BARGAINS BARGAINS IN ALL DEPARTMENTS instead of clues; and the hanging white squares displayed dollar signs instead of question marks.

There had always been strong links between the Twitchpurse and Rubinstein families. Right up to this very date, Ms. Gloria Twitchpurse and Abraham Rubinstein III, the store's owner, were great friends. Both were prominent members of the library's Board of Trustees. So nobody was greatly surprised that Saturday morning to see the Rubinstein Department Store van parked outside the building.

The only question mark in the earliest comers' minds arose when they saw Rubinstein's brightest young window dresser, Mary Farrell, get out of the van, closely followed by the driver, and that question was, "I wonder what's going on *this* time?"

They had both been carrying cardboard boxes piled high with white material, neatly folded like sheets. The mystery deepened when the driver ran back to the van a second time and came out with the limp body of a man dressed in jeans and T-shirt. He'd draped it over his shoulder in a fireman's lift and rushed up the steps into the library, with Mary holding the door and looking impatient.

Well, now everyone knew what the cloth was all about, having just seen it unfurled, its messages displayed above. But what the body had to do with anything still remained a mystery.

The taller and bulkier of the two men up top leaned over the battlements. "How's it look, Ms. Snell?" he called out in a voice that sounded as if he were speaking through a bullhorn.

Ernest Snerdoff, the library's janitor, had been a Marine Corps drill sergeant and when he raised that voice, everyone within a half-mile radius heard it.

A young woman with golden hair and a bright red shirt stepped from the crowd and gave him a cheery A-okay sign. This was Felicity Snell. "Terrific, Mr. Snerdoff!" she called back, moving off toward the side of the building.

Even as she did this, the second man leaned over the parapet and gave one of the question-mark strings a tug. The card swung clear and displayed its interrogation point more plainly.

The sudden jerky movement disturbed a large black bird that had been roosting nearby and it flew off, cackling noisily.

To some of the onlookers, looking back on the incident later, it seemed like an evil omen.

"That bird must have known what was coming!" they said.

This was the opinion of a kid called J. G. Farrell.

But he wasn't thinking of that at the time. All he said right then was, "Is it okay to go in now, Felicity?"

The librarian turned. "Not until nine-thirty," she said. "There's still another half hour to go. Mary will still be busy. You should be with the others, John. Ready for a final briefing. You're in charge of the Watchdog Squad, don't forget."

She continued on her way to the old mobile library van in the far corner of the parking lot. Mr. Hayes, the Chief Librarian, had turned it over to her for use as the newly formed Junior Mystery Club's headquarters. There was an excited cheer from the group of kids waiting outside as she approached. A girl was doing cartwheels all around the van. Another was doing her best to keep up with her. A worried-looking boy was doing his best to keep up with a beagle tugging on a leash. The dog was yapping joyously, as if he took the words Watchdog Squad personally and couldn't wait to start.

This nearly caused disaster even at that early stage. The dog began to run around Felicity's legs. Any other person might have been tripped, but not Felicity. She skipped and leaped through the twists and loops of the snaking leash with the easy agility of the circus acrobat she'd once trained herself to be during her under-cover detective career.

J.G. called out, "I'll be right there!" as if all the cheers had been for him.

But he veered off at the corner and headed for the main door. He couldn't resist it. He was itching to see just what kind of job his sister was making of the assignment. She may have been highly praised for her displays of Easter Bonnets, Halloween Fun, Yuletide Cheer, Summer Fashions, and stuff like that in the windows of Rubinstein's.

But *this* had to do with clues to a mystery and, when it came to mysteries, J.G. Farrell was the expert in that family, thank you very much. He couldn't wait to see what mistakes his sister was making. And, of course, to be on hand to put her right!

Maybe she wouldn't thank him for it, but so what? Nothing like that ever put J.G. off when he'd made up his mind. The other kids used to call him "Jump-the-Gun" Farrell and said that was what the J.G. really stood for, rather than John Gerrit. But so what again? Felicity Snell herself recognized his abilities, didn't she? She'd put him charge of the Watchdog Squad, hadn't she?

So, with his head buzzing and swarming with such notions and good intentions, he passed under the swinging question marks and pushed his way into the lobby.

Meanwhile, the Watchdog Squad stuff could wait. Felicity was only going to go through their duties in making sure the contest ran smoothly, seeing that no one was cheated, and telling them what to watch out for. Maybe *other* members of the squad needed to be instructed, but not J.G. Things like that came naturally to *him*. Instinctively.

No sweat. . . .

2

The Body in the Library

Even as Ernest Snerdoff had been helping the guy from Rubinstein's fix the banners, he'd started to have doubts. It was as if the unfurled message had not been GREAT ONE-DAY CLUEFINDERS CONTEST but GREAT ONE-DAY LIBRARY-WRECKERS SPREE.

As the banner spread out with that almighty clap, it struck him that this might turn out to be nothing less than an open invitation for mayhem and mischief. An invitation to every young hood in West Milbury.

Why, he'd just seen one of them sidle away from the crowd below and head for the main entrance! One he knew from past experience. A mischief-maker supreme. One who obviously just couldn't wait to get started.

Ernest Snerdoff lost no time in getting to the lobby. Just in time to see the kid peering in at the window of the Junior Department door and try the handle.

"Hold it right there, pilgrim!" he barked.

His voice echoed around the lobby. It bounced off the glass-paneled doors of the other departments and the black-and-white tiled floor he'd so recently cleaned.

The kid jumped, startled.

He glanced hurriedly at the floor, wondering if he'd brought in some mud on his shoes and messed up some of those sparkling white squares. But it had been a fine morning and there wasn't a single smear on those tiles.

Besides, that wasn't what the giant ex-Marine was glaring at as he towered over him. He was glaring down at J.G. himself, as if *he* was the smear of crud that defaced that marble hall.

J.G. shuddered slightly as he thought of the Marine battle hymn that Snerdoff used to sing in his (rare) happier moments while he squeegeed that very floor:

From the halls of Montezuma

To the shores of Tripoli . . .

Then the boy pulled himself together. After all, what could the guy *do* to him? He was just a kid, wasn't he, doing nobody any harm? A guy could come in to speak with his own sister, couldn't he? Even if it was before opening hours? Especially when the sister was doing the library a big favor. And probably doing it wrong.

So he blinked politely up at the giant, with his dark, smooth crew cut presented as if for the inspection and approval of the owner of the white, bristly crew cut looming over him. J.G. was tall for his thirteen years, but it still caused a crick in his neck to do this at such close quarters.

There was something about the politeness of that blink that made Snerdoff calm down a little. Maybe it was the kid's odd eyes: the left one brown; the right, a silvery gray. Some kind of mesmerizing effect, maybe. Also the neatness of that crew cut that showed off a high, smooth white forehead and gave the kid a brainy look.

Then Snerdoff found himself bridling again. The upraised black eyebrows gave the brat a snooty look, a cocky, know-it-all look. He'd seen that type too often, back at Boot Camp. Always looking promising, alert, keen—but they were very deceptive. The kind that could throw the whole battalion into horrible disarray. Marching out of step. Dropping rifles while being inspected by the C.O.

Oh yes! This was worse than a hood. This was a troublemaker. A downright bad-news troublemaker!

"Whadda ya want here, pilgrim? Your sister's busy, can't ya see?"

"Yes, sir. But I've got to have a word with her right away. Or else . . ."

"Or else nothing, pilgrim! You can read, can't you?"

Snerdoff stabbed a finger the size of a bratwurst at a notice taped to the door's glass panel. This one:

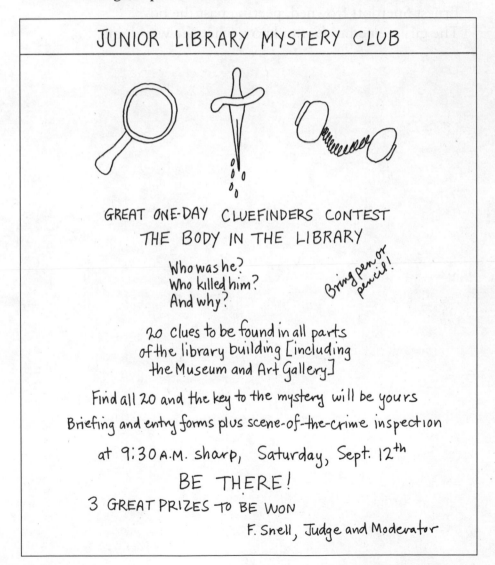

JUNIOR LIBRARY MYSTERY CLUB

GREAT ONE-DAY CLUEFINDERS CONTEST
THE BODY IN THE LIBRARY

Who was he?
Who killed him?
And why?

Bring pen or pencil!

20 clues to be found in all parts
of the library building [including
the Museum and Art Gallery]

Find all 20 and the key to the mystery will be yours
Briefing and entry forms plus scene-of-the-crime inspection

at 9:30 A.M. sharp, Saturday, Sept. 12th
BE THERE!
3 GREAT PRIZES TO BE WON

F. Snell, Judge and Moderator

The janitor's finger had come to a quivering rest on the words and numbers: 9:30 A.M. *sharp*.

J.G. turned to look through the glass around the edges of the notice.

"But she's doing it all *wrong*, sir!"

Ernest Snerdoff frowned, peering past the boy.

The girl seemed to *him* to know what she was doing. . . .

Mary Prepares the Crime Scene

Mary Farrell was on her knees in front of the counter. She was a good-looking girl, about eighteen years old. She, too, had a high, nicely rounded, brainy forehead and the same upraised eyebrows. But they didn't make *her* look snooty. Maybe it was because of her tiptilted nose. It was too short to look down along at other people, they way J.G. so often seemed to do.

Another difference was that *her* hair was red, just like the hair of her mother, father, and three older sisters. J.G. was the only family member to have black hair. Or odd eyes, for that matter. Mary's eyes were a pleasant hazel green when she opened them wide.

But they were half closed at this moment, deeply concentrated on her work. She was completely engrossed in arranging the body to make it look as if it belonged to someone who'd been hurrying to the phone on the counter to call for help. Someone who'd been struck down savagely before he could make it.

She had already secured the area with a green-and-white striped tape bearing the words WEST MILBURY P.D. CRIME SCENE—PLEASE KEEP BACK. Felicity had obtained it from her friend Detective Delaney. It was neatly draped from three chairs placed strategically near the body.

On the floor, ready for Mary's use, were scissors, Scotch tape, a staple gun and staple cartridge, a chunky piece of chalk and, slightly apart from these, a thick reference book. It wasn't one of those with a brightly colored jacket, about birds, flowers, or animals, like those from the Junior Room shelves. Snerdoff recognized it as a heavy, serious volume from the Main Reference Room upstairs. It had no business being down here, he thought to himself, pressing his lips together in vexation.

Mary's lips were tightly pressed together, too. Partly it was with concentration, but mainly because of the pins she kept clamped in her mouth, ready for use on the job. She was famous for this in West Milbury. Kids often went to watch her at work in Rubinstein's windows. Not only to see the marvelous displays take shape under her nimble fingers. But also—especially the older boys—to try to get her to laugh or to snarl at them to clear off, in the hope of making her drop the pins. This was safe enough when the plate glass stood between Mary and the onlookers. But close up, like at home, it was risky business, as J.G. well knew. Mary could put those pins to deadly use as missiles, spitting them out like darts from a blowpipe! She was—slowly and thoughtfully—*taking* one out now, as she rearranged the folds in the victim's T-shirt—the better to display the gash made by the knife that lay beside the body close to a pool of blood.

It was this blood that had aroused J.G.'s critical instincts.

He peered closer.

Yes. Definitely plastic. Bright red plastic.

He knew it for one of the props owned by the West Milbury Amateur Dramatic Club, of which Mary was a member. Like the dagger itself, which was really made of silver-painted rubber.

Between the gash in the shirt and the dummy's body, Mary was now deftly sliding another, smaller piece of red plastic. This made it look as if there was a horrible deep wound in there, oozing blood.

She plucked another pin from her mouth and gave the shirt another tuck so that the "wound" caught the light and glittered even more gorily. Then, with her head to one side and her eyes still half closed, she rocked back on her heels, the better to see how the effect might look from any spectator's point of view.

"Looks okay to me!" murmured Snerdoff, relieved to see it was plastic and not some messy liquid like catsup that *he'd* have to clean up later.

"I tell you it's all *wrong*!" insisted J.G.

None of this seemed to reach Mary's ears as, still absorbed in her work, she took up the reference book and transferred it carefully to the dummy's outstretched left hand, leaving the title exposed: *World Almanac and Book of Facts*.

Finally, she drew a thick chalk outline around the knife, to match the one she'd made earlier around the body. And, sure enough, it did now look like a genuine murder scene.

If it hadn't been for that shiny pool of "blood," J.G. decided. And the victim's limbs. They could use some rearranging, to make the guy look as if he'd died writhing in greater agony and terror.

He turned back to Ernest Snerdoff as the janitor said, "Wrong? *How* wrong?"

"She's using a fake pool of blood!" said J.G. "Plastic."

"I can *see* that!" grunted Snerdoff, still looking relieved.

"But it *looks* like it's still wet! The stabbing's supposed to have been done during the night. The blood would be drying up by now!"

"So what?"

The janitor was now curious. He glanced at the plastic pool.

"So she ought to be using gravy or something," said J.G. "Some-

21

thing brownish. The way blood looks when it dries. Any fool knows *that*!"

"Not on *my* carpet!" growled Snerdoff.

"But it would brush off, leaving the rug looking like new. If she used brown poster paint . . ."

The janitor made a sudden gargling noise—half yelp, half snarl. There had been accidents with poster paints in here before. Usually when Felicity Snell was illustrating some story and the kids crowded too close to the open jar.

"Over my dead body!" he growled.

"No, sir, Mr. Snerdoff!" said J.G., blinking innocently again. "Over the *dummy's* dead body! That's the whole idea! To make it look real. To"—J.G. remembered something he'd once read—"to *strike horror into the hearts of the onlookers!*"

Something seemed to have struck horror into the tough old leathery heart of Ernest Snerdoff as, with a sudden rattle, the door was unlocked and flung open.

"Looking for *me*, Mr. Snerdoff?" Mary said in a strangely menacing voice—not loud but extremely vicious—like the buzz of a queen bee disturbed in her hive.

She was speaking through what remained of the mouthful of pins.

"Stay where you are, you!"

The last words—vibrating with fury—were aimed at J.G.

So were the pins.

He hurriedly ducked behind Ernest Snerdoff.

4

The Key to the Contest?

But J.G. needn't have bothered.

Mary held her fire.

Better leave the talking to Snerdoff, he decided.

"J-just doing my duty, miss!" the man stammered, taken aback by her quiet ferocity. "Makin' sure you don't get interrupted."

"Well I *have* been interrupted, haven't I?" she snapped. "So how about *that*?"

"I . . . I . . . uh . . . I guess I . . ." The giant was lifting his right hand to his head in a feeble salute, cowed and confused.

His eyes flitted about the room, at the ceiling, the floor, at the sprawled dummy, the chalk outline, the dagger, the pool of blood. Anywhere but the girl's eyes.

He was remembering the look on the face of the Rubinstein's driver. Less than half an hour ago, the guy had been shaking, positively trembling with fear, or anger, or both. He, too, had just been on the receiving end of one of Mary Farrell's outbursts.

It was when Ernest Snerdoff had gone to collect the banners. He'd just caught the tail end of the storm as the guy was backing out of the Junior Room.

"Who d'you think *you* are, Carl Green?" she was saying. "*I'm* the only qualified window dresser here!"

"I . . . I . . . was only trying to help!"

"Well go try to help Mr. Snerdoff here fix the banners. See if you can get *that* right!"

"Sure, right away, Mary. No problem, no—"

"Go!"

Mary was already focusing her attention back on the dummy.

The pale, skinny, wimpish young driver took the steps to the top floor so fast that even the janitor had to work hard to keep up.

It turned out that the guy's only crime had been to bring along a new raincoat from Rubinstein's menswear department to dress the dummy in. Without consulting Mary first.

As Snerdoff now glanced around the Junior Room, still avoiding those angry hazel-green eyes, he caught sight of that raincoat. It was bundled up in a far corner near the kindergarten shelves where Mary had hurled it.

It had landed on the small table where Felicity displayed the large scrapbook of the kids' own stories that she'd written down and illustrated herself. The impact had knocked the table askew and now the coat looked like another dead thing—the corpse of some octopus-like monster, completely covering that large brightly colored book, with the sleeves and the ends of the belt dangling limply over the edge of the table.

The janitor breathed a whole lot easier when Mary turned back to her brother.

"And what do *you* want?" she said, the pins still in her mouth.

"A word . . . that . . . that's all," J.G. replied, very cautiously.

"About what?"

"The blood."

"What blood?"

J.G. seemed to take some courage from this. He even smiled.

"You do right to ask, Sis." Now he was looking more like his normal snooty self. "Because, of course, *this* isn't blood. This red plastic stuff. What you need is something more like blood that's already dried or drying. A browner color. Rusty, kind of. Maybe a poster paint that shade."

Ernest Snerdoff groaned softly.

Mary gazed at her brother with amazement. "Now let's just get this straight," she said slowly. "You're telling me to use rust-colored paint to make it look like *old* blood?"

"Well, sure. Like it had been spilled some hours earlier."

"Instead of this perfectly realistic magenta plastic pool?" Mary's voice was rising again. "Which has been good enough for dozens of stage productions? . . . Get a life, junior!"

"She's right, pilgrim," said the janitor, hurriedly. "We don't want no mess! And she *is* the expert."

"Thank you, Mr. Snerdoff!" said Mary. "I'm glad to see someone's got some true dramatic taste around here."

J.G. raised his eyebrows higher. "I'm thinking of what makes good *detective* sense, not what might look good in some dumb play!"

His sister sneered right back. "Well anyway, for your information, I cleared the plastic with Ms. Snell first, over the phone last night. She said it sounded *great*."

"There you are, pilgrim!" said the janitor.

Then, glancing down at the rug, he clapped his hand to his chest.

But no, it wasn't *his* name tag that was lying on the floor. That was still pinned to his shirt. But it was *a* name tag. With the library logo.

He bent to take a closer look and saw:

He frowned as he reached out to pick it up.

Arnold Cripps? He'd never heard of the guy.

Assistant janitor? He, Ernest Snerdoff, was the only janitor there.

"Leave it lie!" snapped Mary Farrell, before his fingers had touched it. "That's another of my rejects, like the coat over there. I was going to pin it to the dummy's shirt until I realized that was something *else* he wouldn't be wearing. Not off duty, late last night."

"Good thinking, Sis!" said J.G. cheerfully, completely relaxed again. "Now you're thinking like us detectives."

Mary gave him a withering look. She hated being addressed as Sis. And this was twice in the last few minutes!

But her brother was continuing to speak his own detective mind, fully in orbit now.

"What's all this about the coat?" he said. "Why *shouldn't* he be wearing a coat off duty?" He was so fully in orbit that he'd pulled a pipe from his pocket. It was an old one that his father had thrown out. J.G. never used it for smoking, but he liked waving it about when the investigating mood was upon him. It made him feel like Sherlock Holmes and some other great detectives he'd seen on TV or read about. It irritated Mary almost beyond endurance. Even Snerdoff tended to go cross-eyed with suspicion and annoyance whenever he saw J.G. toting it in the library.

Mary was only just managing to keep her cool. But she brought herself to answer her brother's question. Her lip curled in a superior smile. "Because, Mr. Ace Detective, as I explained to that other klutz, Carl Green, it was very warm last night. And that coat is winter weight, extra long." She sniffed. "Apart from being a seven-hundred-dollar Burberry that no assistant janitor could ever afford."

"Anyway," said Snerdoff, "who says he . . . it's supposed to be the assistant janitor?"

"Felicity Snell says, Mr. Snerdoff," replied Mary.

"It's in the script, sir," said J.G. "Arnold Cripps is just a made-up name. Fictitious. Me, I'd have given the dummy *your* name. And made it look like you. And tattooed its arms like yours. And . . ."

"*What* script?" Snerdoff looked alarmed.

"The story behind the contest," said J.G. "Ms. Snell wrote it. She gave Mary a copy as a guide to setting up the scene. Right, Sis?"

"Sure," said Mary, warily. "Here . . ."

She fished out a typewritten sheet from the bunch of articles on the floor. Ernest Snerdoff put on his glasses and read:

① ②
/ The name of the killer is / Frank X. Rollins. He had a heated
③ ④
argument / late at night with the deceased / Arnold Cripps, an assistant
⑤
janitor at the local library, / over which was the highest mountain
⑥
in North America. / Cripps said Mount McKinley, Rollins said Mount
⑦ ⑧
Logan. / They bet each other $500. / To settle it, Cripps took Rollins
⑨ ⑩
to the library, / letting them in with his duplicate key. / Then
⑪ ⑫
Cripps showed Rollins the / Reference Room almanac / that proved
⑬ ⑭
him right. / Rollins then got mad, / saying he'd been deliberately
⑮ ⑯
set up. They / fought fiercely all over the library, / ending up
⑰ ⑱
in the Junior Department / where Rollins finally / stabbed Cripps,
⑲ ⑳
killing him. / He is now serving a / life sentence for the murder.

"What's all these numbers?" asked Snerdoff.

"Beats *me*," said Mary, shrugging. "They were already written in."

J.G. gave the pipe a warning wave.

"Ah, now that's the key to the contest, sir! You see, there'll be twenty clues. Twenty cards numbered One through Twenty. They'll be hidden all over the building. Like it says there." J.G. pointed to the notice on the door.

Snerdoff nodded. This was what had been worrying him. "So what happens? I suppose the kids collect the cards as they find them?"

"Not exactly . . . ," J.G. began.

But the janitor's fears were beginning to take control. "And then what?" he went on. "Do they go around snatching each other's cards to make up a full set? Do the little ones get mugged for their cards by the big ones? Do the little kids' big brothers go after the muggers to mug *them*?"

Squabbles. Fights. Mayhem. Pandemonium. Riots. Complete breakdown of law and order.

Snerdoff could see it all happening in his library!

J.G. was shaking the pipe. "No, sir . . . You've got it all wrong . . ."

"And what about kids who come in late?" the janitor continued, getting more and more worked up. "After most of the cards have been collected? Huh? Looking for cards that aren't even there no more? Huh? *Huh?* Turning the place over and finding zilch?"

Snerdoff could see books being snatched from shelves and tossed to one side—some even ripped apart in the fruitless search. More mayhem. More squabbles. The library a complete disaster area.

"No, sir, Mr. Snerdoff!" J.G. had to shout to break in on this nightmare scenario. "They don't *collect* the clue cards. They have to leave them exactly where they find them!"

Snerdoff gaped. He could hardly believe his ears. This sounded much too good to be true.

"So . . . so how will Ms. Snell know if the kids have *really* found them and aren't lying through their teeth when they say they have?"

"Because they simply make a note of the words or names marked on the cards."

Still not believing his luck, the janitor said, "What words? What names?"

"These." J.G. tapped the script. "The numbers are here, right? Well, the words or names are the ones next to the numbers. Like for Number One, the word is *The*. For Number Two, it's a name, *Frank*. Number Three, the word's *late*. For Four, another name, *Arnold*—and so on, through to Twenty."

Ernest Snerdoff suddenly relaxed. At last he could see the solution to all his fears.

No fights. No muggings. No riots.

Bliss . . .

"Gee!" he said. "That Ms. Snell, she thinks of everything!"

"So now that *that's* settled," said Mary, who'd just about come to the end of her patience, "how about leaving me in peace to get on with the crime scene?"

"Better do like she says, fellas!" said a voice from the door. "She's got that look in her eyes."

It was the Rubinstein driver again. With his timidly blinking sandy eyelashes, in that sandy-colored smock worn by all Rubinstein workpeople (except top executives and artistic window dressers), he looked totally insignificant and no-account. The only noticeable splash of color was the dark red Rubinstein logo embroidered on the smock.

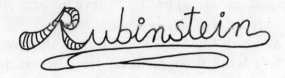

Rubinstein

"Yes," said another, more familiar voice, as Felicity Snell stepped into the doorway. "Come along, John. The crowd's building up outside. We have less than fifteen minutes before the contest opens."

Other faces came pressing forward, behind her. J.G. recognized Tim Kowalski, Freddie Fisher, Holly Jenks, and other members of the Watchdog Squad.

"Boy!" gasped Mary, giving him a shove. "Is that all the time left? . . . Out! Out! Out! *Now* already!"

5

The Contestants Gather

Fifteen minutes later, at 9:30 sharp, the crowd was gathered behind the green-and-white crime scene tape in the Junior Room. They were mostly kids, drawn from all parts of the town. The Junior Library Mystery Club's invitation had appeared on the bulletin boards of supermarkets and other stores as well as in schools, church halls, and even pinball and video game arcades. Freddie Fisher, who had designed the notice, made sure of that!

Some kids had been attracted by Freddie's picture of the gorily dripping dagger; others, by the handcuffs and magnifying glass; and still others by the mention of the Mystery Club itself, which they'd only just heard about. All were hooked by the idea of a *Cluefinders* Contest, and the words "The Body in the Library" had clinched it for everyone, as did the name F. Snell at the bottom.

And now, they weren't disappointed. There, on the floor, was that body sprawled in its own blood. And there, full of life, was F. Snell herself sitting on the edge of the counter—her favorite storytelling perch—ready to tell them about the contest, and the clues, and the prizes, exactly as promised!

This was going to be good!

This was going to be *great*!

This was going to be something else!

As they pressed forward, eager to know and see more, not one of these would-be prizewinning sleuths seemed to notice the unusually strained look on Felicity's face. . . .

True, there were several more strained faces present among the adults standing behind the counter or along the sides of the room toward the front. But there was nothing unusual about some of *them*. Ernest Snerdoff always looked strained when there were kids around. Nor was there anything unusual about the suspicious glint behind the gold-rimmed glasses of Ms. Emily Fitch, the Reference Librarian. This was the lady who fiercely refused to let anyone under sixteen enter her room on the second floor uninvited or without permission.

Mr. Hayes, the Chief Librarian, looked relaxed though. There was usually a smile brightening his dark African American face, but right now it was broader than ever. Some of these kids had never set foot in his building before. But now that they had, they might stay on to become regulars.

If all went well!

He'd heard some of the staff murmuring their misgivings. But with Felicity in charge, nothing *serious* could go wrong, could it?

Or could it?

For all his relaxed appearance, his fingers were tightly crossed. After all, his job might depend on this. Until Felicity came, only a few months earlier, the Junior Department had been losing members, and there'd been rumors that the trustees were thinking of letting him go. Now, thanks to Felicity's efforts, membership figures were climbing again, and the success of this contest might boost those figures higher still.

Ms. Gloria Twitchpurse, standing at the side of the room, was looking pleased anyway. Chairperson of the trustees, the way *she* felt could be very important. So could the way another of the trustees present felt. Mr. Abraham Rubinstein III was standing next to her and he, too, had every reason to look pleased. *And why not?* Mr. Hayes was thinking. The two Rubinstein employees who'd set up the murder scene and the banners outside had done a great job—the girl in particular.

Suddenly a shiver ran down the Chief Librarian's back, freezing this stream of pleasant thoughts.

Gloria Twitchpurse had given a little stifled scream, and Mr. Rubinstein had rolled his eyes and muttered a rumbling "Oh, no!"

A kid had stepped beyond the green-and-white tape. A nervous, nosy, hyperactive nine-year-old named Benny Stockler. Mr. Hayes remembered him mainly from a Pet Club meeting up in the Natural History Museum last year. He'd brought along his pet ferret. Just when everything was going well, that ferret had slipped its collar and gotten in among the rabbits. Purely accidental, according to the shocked and dismayed Benny, but creating uproar and mayhem all the same. "Matilda," the kid had called that ferret. Mr. Hayes always remembered that. It sounded like Attila. . . .

Now something similar seemed to be happening again.

Benny had gone forward to get a closer look at the reference book in the dummy's left hand. Unfortunately he'd been startled by the janitor's harsh whisper—"Get out of there, pilgrim! *Now!*"— and he'd tripped over the dummy's right foot. As he lost his footing, he made a grab at the counter. And as he made the wild grab, he almost knocked over the cut glass vase of wildflowers that Felicity's aide, Elaine, had placed there.

It all happened in a flash. And in another flash, merging with the first, Felicity reached out and caught the vase. Just in the nick of time. With her left hand, too!

A collective sigh of relief went up from some of the adults.

But it hadn't done much to ease the tension of the doubters.

If that vase had crashed to the floor, breaking into fragments, with a couple of pints of water splashing all over—carrying with it the black-eyed Susans, clover, and baby's breath that Elaine had so lovingly arranged—who knows what pandemonium might have broken out?

Well, what the heck! thought Mr. Hayes. *You can't make an omelette without breaking a few eggs!*

All the same, it had been touch and go.

6

Felicity to the Rescue Again

The incident caused a rise in the general noise level. Naturally, the kids began to comment to one another on the sheer swiftness of Felicity's reaction.

Then, adding to this, came the popping of flashbulbs as a couple of photographers got busy. One had been sent by a local paper to cover this unusual event and catch all the action, if any—and now it looked as if the readers weren't going to be disappointed.

Other kids, inspired by Benny, were already investigating for themselves. A few had hit on the idea of using their entry forms—tossing them up in the air and getting them to float or skim across the police line, giving themselves an excuse to cross over. This soon caught on.

The general rise in the fuss level even communicated itself through the open windows and out across the parking lot to the dog that Spencer Curtis had had to leave tied to the bumper of the old library van.

Then Benny's sobs began to fill the air.

Once again, Felicity acted fast. Jumping lightly off the counter, she landed next to the body, snatched up the reference book, and said in a loud, clear, carrying voice, "Yes, Benny. This *is* an important clue. You were right to be so interested."

Benny stopped dead in mid-sob. And when he realized these kind words were addressed exclusively to him, his face lit up. It lit up so suddenly, shining through the tears, it was a wonder there wasn't a rainbow.

The girls in the audience loved it. This was one of the great things about Felicity, they seemed to be thinking. She could make a nervous little kid light up in a flash.

But just then, there was another interruption.

It was made by an older boy, as pale and twitchy-looking as Benny. He was a stranger and obviously new to the town. He'd been standing next to a plump, blond, well-dressed woman who kept putting her hand on his shoulder, which he kept shaking off. She, herself, was standing next to Gloria Twitchpurse. Sometimes she put her other hand through Ms. Twitchpurse's arm. They were obviously close friends.

At Benny's blunder and Felicity's rescue, the new kid seemed to pick up interest. And now he'd slid away from the woman's side and *he'd crossed the police line himself*! Even Snerdoff had been taken by surprise. There were gasps from others, but the kid didn't take any notice as he stooped to the fake pool of blood, prodded it with a finger, then picked it up.

"It isn't real, Mom!" he said. "It's only a piece of crummy plastic!"

"Come out of there, Orville darling!" said the woman.

A flashbulb popped and lit up the boy.

And that seemed to be the signal for the pandemonium that Felicity had only just managed to avoid minutes earlier.

"Aw, *Orville*, darling!" jeered one of the older boys in a loud, breaking voice. "Do what Momma says!"

"Mustn't touch, Orville!" sang out another.

"Yeah, don't be awful, Orville!" added a third.

Then came a complete chorus of "Awful Orville! Awful Orville!"

Ernest Snerdoff was looking fit to be tied as his worst fears began to take shape.

Then a voice cut through the din.

"Tell us about the clues, Felicity!"

It was none other than J.G.'s! There was a strange glint in his eyes, both the gray and the brown. And the pipe was in his hand again.

"Yes. And tell them about us Watchdogs," another voice called out—this time a girl's. Ruth Fisher, J.G.'s one-time bitter enemy, was now a staunch deputy on the newly formed squad.

Giving the two kids a grateful glance, Felicity hopped back onto the counter.

"Yes! Listen up, everybody! Pick up those entry forms, cool it, and pay attention! Here's what you need to know if you want to win a prize!"

She said this with another glance. This was at Mr. Rubinstein—a hopeful glance this time. The department store owner had been looking as if he was beginning to enjoy this even more.

"Yes!" he said. "There'll be ten *extra* consolation prizes as of now. Rubinstein gift vouchers—to use in any department of the store!"

This produced a burst of cheering.

Their attention was now not only riveted but *rapt*.

Once again Mr. Hayes began to breathe easier.

7

Benny's Clue—with Important Details about the Other Nineteen

"Okay," said Felicity briskly, "there are twenty clues. Each clue is in the form of a card. None of them will be completely hidden. Each will be just visible to those with sharp eyes."

At this, about fifty pairs of eyes narrowed or squinted in an effort to look keen and sharp.

"They've been left in various rooms and other places throughout the building. Remember, it looks as if it all started upstairs, in the Reference Room, judging by the book the victim was clutching."

All eyes switched from the dummy to Ms. Fitch, whose face turned a dusky red. Then, everyone's eyes went back to Felicity again as she held up the almanac.

"There was a fight—probably over something in this book—a fight that broke off as the victim fled. And then there was a chase, with the victim being stalked by the killer. Ending up here, in this room."

Felicity was looking at the body. No fidgeting now. Felicity's storytelling magic had them all under its spell. Even Ernest Snerdoff, whose mouth was hanging open to prevent his breath from rasping too loudly through the hairs in his nostrils.

"The chase," Felicity continued, "must have gone on through the early hours. During that time the victim will have passed through places like the Adult Lending Department, cowering behind the bookstacks there, or in the museum rooms upstairs or the Art Gallery. He might have tried to conceal himself behind a mummy case, or a statue, or a tapestry hanging from a wall."

One of the kids sneezed. This sudden noise caused Orville's mother to give a little scream. She had looked all along like a complete bundle of nerves, and Orville didn't make things any better by glaring up and groaning, "*Mother!*"

"The victim might," Felicity hurried on, "even have stood very still, in the shadows, pretending to be a statue himself."

There was dead silence again.

"Anyway," Felicity said, holding up an entry form, "you'll find on here a list of the places he passed through, leaving clues. These." She pointed out the list, typed in red:

```
            Likely Locations

        [4] Junior Room
        [3] Reference Room
        [2] Adult Lending Department
        [2] Video Department
        [2] Newspaper and Magazine Room
        [3] Museum Rooms
        [2] Art Gallery
        [2] Third Floor
```

"The numbers in brackets," she explained, "refer to the number of clues left in each location. . . ." She paused. "Now, about the Third Floor—the victim might have gone hoping to find refuge up there. But his luck ran out. The Staff Room was locked. Mr. Hayes's Office was locked. No time to find the right keys—the killer was getting closer all the time. So no clues inside these rooms, which is why they're at the head of this other list."

She tapped the entry form, where the typing, also in red, stated:

<u>STRICTLY OFF LIMITS</u>

* Staff Room
* The Chief Librarian's Office
* Basement (all parts)
* Nonpublic areas for use of staff only
  (E.g., behind counters in all departments)
* <u>The Local Collection in Reference Room</u>
  (At the special request of Ms. Emily Fitch)

Ms. Fitch coughed anxiously. "Ms. Snell, you did say you would—"

"Of course." Felicity cut in. "I was just about to mention it, Ms. Fitch. Please make a special note of that last item on the list, everyone. . . . There are no clues to be found in the Reference Room Local Collection. That's the smaller room at the back. Okay?"

There was a general murmur. Most of the kids wouldn't have been surprised to learn that Ms. Fitch had put a dreadful curse on it anyway.

"But clues could have been left in the corridors near any of these places," Felicity continued. "The victim would probably be bleeding by now from wounds picked up in the first bout of fighting. Before the killer pulled the knife."

All eyes turned again to the dagger beside the "corpse."

"And now," said Felicity, "let me show you the actual Number One Clue that Benny spotted."

Felicity held up the thick almanac and pointed to its spine, where, peeping out from the tip was the merest strip of bright red card. Drawing it out slowly, Felicity revealed it was the size of a calling card. She held it out for the kids to get a better look and turned it to show both sides.

It was completely blank except for the number *1* in the top corner of one side and the word *The*.

"So here's your starter clue," said Felicity. "Brought to you by Benny Stockler, with his compliments. All right, Benny?"

The kid had been looking bewildered, but when he realized everyone was looking at him, including the Chief Librarian and Mr. Rubinstein, who were both smiling with approval, he stood up and gave them all a huge swooping bow.

"So, go ahead," said Felicity to the crowd. "Copy that word on the dotted line next to the number on the entry form and you're in business."

Everyone was looking at the forms again and the numbers typed out neatly:

1.	6.	11.	16. . . . . .
2.	7.	12.	17. . . . . .
3.	8.	13.	18. . . . . .
4.	9.	14.	19. . . . . .
5.	10.	15.	20. . . . . .

Some kids were already writing out Benny's gift word in the space next to the number *1*.

In their eagerness, the word was coming in all shapes and sizes.

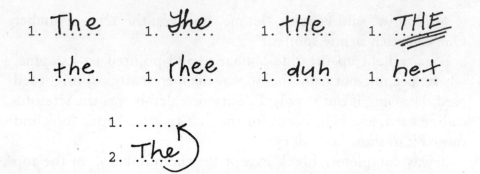

1. The   1. The   1. tHe   1. THE

1. the   1. rhee   1. duh   1. het

1. .....
2. The

"Now, all you have to do is find the other nineteen and do the same," said Felicity, wincing a little as she read some of the examples.

Then her eyes twinkled. She'd spotted some other spaces that had been filled out with check marks.

"The correct word will prove you really *have* found the clue. *Anyone* could put a check mark there, whether they really find a card or not."

Some of the wise guys who'd been putting in check marks were busy, even as she spoke, erasing or scratching them out frantically. J.G. wasn't the only kid in town who couldn't resist jumping the gun!

"And now an important reminder," said Felicity. "When you've found a card and written down the word, put that card back exactly where you found it, ready for others to spot. And to make sure nobody cheats and hides the card completely where it can't be seen at all . . ."

Felicity slowly pushed the red card back into the spine of the almanac until it was totally out of sight. The ears of some of those watching turned as red as the card itself, showing the way *their* minds had been working.

"Or if they do this by accident, not meaning to cheat . . . then don't worry. Members of the Junior Mystery Club's Watchdog

Squad will be close at hand to see that the cards are put back in the right places."

This was greeted by a burst of clapping. Not only from the kids, glad to hear this news, but also from staff members relieved to hear that there'd be less likelihood of noisy accusations and protests of innocence breaking the peace of the library as the search for clues got under way.

Felicity glanced around. "Okay, squad!" she said. "Step up and let everyone see who you are!"

8

The Watchdog Squad on Parade

So the Watchdog Squad got to enjoy the huge privilege of stepping behind the green-and-white tape. First across, right into the very thick of the crime scene, was J.G. He lost no time in bending over the body and probing at the gaping wound with the pipe stem as if searching for a bullet.

"It's been *stabbed*, you jerk, not *shot*!" hissed his sister. She'd been standing at the side with some of the other onlookers. She couldn't bear to see her work being messed with like this.

J.G. took no notice whatever.

Freddie Fisher and Tim Kowalski looked as if they were enjoying it almost as much as J.G., out there in full view. More, even, in Freddie's case. He'd taken his position right in front of Felicity. And as she picked up a large sheet of paper, he seemed to know what was coming. He was only a rather undersized, skinny kid of eleven, but his chest could swell with as much pride as anyone's.

"The squad members here are *not* spies, or snoopers, or finks," Felicity told the audience, who'd already started to mutter their opinions. "They're here to help the contest run smoothly. As you see, they all have ID tags, especially designed by Freddie Fisher." She held up the sheet of paper. "Here's a blown-up copy."

As a murmur of admiration rose, Freddie's chest seemed to expand by a good three inches.

And why not, when he could produce this:

The eyes had been Freddie's idea. Coming like that, under the library's regular logo, they made the peaks of the *M* look like pricked-up ears.

"Watchdog's ears!" he had said. "Get it?"

Holly Jenks had shuddered and said, "More like wolf's ears. A *Watch Wolf's.*"

But Felicity herself had liked it. Even J.G. had. "Nice work, kid!" he'd announced, immediately grabbing a spare tag for himself.

He was wearing the spare now. After rapidly personalizing the eyes by coloring the right one gray and the left one brown, he'd pinned the first tag high on his chest and the second one on the back of his shirt collar.

"To show any wannabe cheats they've got a guy with eyes in the back of his head to deal with here!" he'd announced.

Holly Jenks was wearing hers almost completely concealed, pinned to the waistband of her jeans. But it wasn't because she was hoping to entrap some unwitting kid into cheating, mistakenly thinking there wasn't a Watchdog around.

It was because she was wearing a new red shirt.

"Real silk like Felicity's, and I don't want to spoil it by sticking a pin through it," she had explained.

"Huh!" J.G. had replied. "You're not very observant. Felicity pins *hers* to her silk shirts!"

The rest of the squad were wearing their tags the regular way—up front and proudly, even boastfully. Julie Fisher, who could walk on her hands as well as most folk could walk on their feet, did pin hers upside down at first.

"I might have to walk on my hands to get a better look at clues on the floor," she explained.

But her older sister, Ruth, wasn't buying that. "Fix it properly! This is a very serious mission! Okay?"

So, reluctantly, Julie had fixed it properly.

The only Watchdog whose positioning of the tag was in some doubt was Spencer Curtis. He still hadn't entered the crime scene area and his back was turned to the audience.

The barking of the dog had grown louder and Spencer was pushing his way to the window at the side of the room.

"Excuse me," he said, to Mary Farrell and the driver. Mary was still glaring at her brother, who still prodded at her handiwork with his pipe. The driver was just keeping quiet, trying to steer well clear of any more trouble. "That's my dog, Sweets, down there and I'm just checking." The driver moved out of Spencer's way, grudgingly at first. "Sweets knows I've brought some of his favorite candy." Spencer patted his pocket. "Peanut brittle."

"Really?" murmured the man, beginning to look interested, as if glad of anything that would take Mary's mind off her brother and help her cool off.

"Yeah. It's why we call him Sweets," said Spencer, looking out to where the beagle, ears flapping, was prancing about on its leash, which was still looped around the old library van's back bumper. He grinned. "He isn't *exactly* a regular-looking watchdog. Not with *those* ears. But he's very intelligent. I bet his sixth sense

46

tells him we're all about ready to go, up here."

"Is that a fact?" murmured the man.

"Yeah," said Spencer, who always liked talking about his dog. "If these clues was all pieces of peanut brittle instead of cards, he'd a found 'em all by now. He'd a ate all the evidence before the contest even started!"

The dog's barking was getting more frantic. Almost as if Sweets could hear what Spencer was saying.

The proud owner was thinking of making this observation to the sympathetic listener, when Felicity's voice cut through.

"If you're ready, Spencer . . . ?"

"Gosh, yes!" he gasped. "Excuse me, sir," he said, snapping off a piece of the candy and popping it in his mouth. "Gotta go on duty. . . ."

"And now," Felicity was saying to the crowd, as Spencer stepped into the arena, getting withering looks from the squad's leader, "one thing more. Some clues will be fairly easy to spot, like Benny's. Others will be much harder. I've used gold cards for the harder ones. Golden yellow. In all, there'll be fifteen red cards and five gold."

The audience grew quiet again. Only Sweets's barking broke the silence.

"And to help you," said Felicity, holding up an entry form, "I've given some extra guidance with the golds. Sort of clues *about* clues. Here, under the heading *Extra Help*. For example, the hardest of all, Number Twenty. I'll just read it out. . . ." She went on more slowly, *"Go right to the top for this one."*

There was a buzz of voices and a rustle of paper as the kids bent their heads to read this puzzler for themselves. The brighter ones were just getting around to figuring it must have meant that Number Twenty was somewhere up on the Third Floor, when a voice rang out:

"*I've got it!*"

Everyone looked up, startled.

It was Benny Stockler again.

He was standing on one of the chairs over which the police tape had been draped—a chair slap in front of Mr. Hayes.

Benny's sharp eyes had happened to see the man's smile widen when Felicity had read out the clue about the clue. In less than a couple of seconds, he'd clambered onto the chair. And as he stared at the name tag, "Thaddeus Hayes, Chief Librarian," a grin spread over his own face.

"Gotcha!" he said.

Mr. Hayes's smile had shrunk out of sight. "Huh?"

"Yes, sir," said Benny. "It's *you*! It's *there* on your ID!"

Benny was stabbing a finger at the words, "Chief Librarian."

"That makes *you* the top person here, right, sir?"

"I . . . I . . ."

"Well *I've* come right to the top and I've spotted it."

"Spotted what?" asked Mr. Hayes, faintly.

"The hardest clue of all. Shining from behind your handkerchief. The gold card!"

The kid reached up and with a quick flourish whipped the white handkerchief out from Mr. Hayes's breast pocket.

There was a gasp from everyone watching. One big fat collective horrified gasp. Followed by a smaller one, almost a squeak.

The smaller one had escaped from Benny.

Sure, that was a golden yellow card that had been lurking behind the handkerchief.

But it wasn't one of Felicity's clue cards. It was a card issued by Slim's Shoe Repairs to inform Mr. Hayes that his best shoes were ready to be collected.

"Good try, Benny!" said the top librarian, recovering first and grinning.

"Yes! Better luck next time, Benny!" sang out Felicity. "And next time don't make such a fuss when you find a clue. You don't want the others to find it that easily and maybe beat you to a prize, do you? Keep it to yourself and note it quietly, the way all *real* detectives do."

Coming from someone who'd actually been a real detective that was advice even Benny couldn't ignore. His head had been hanging, but now he lifted it, and murmured, "Yes, ma'am!"

"Good!" Felicity jumped down from the counter and clapped her hands. "And now, go to it, all of you. Remember, the first one to find all twenty clues and write in the correct words, is the winner!"

She didn't have to say another thing.

Benny's little drama had whetted all their appetites.

They were raring to go.

9

The Biggest Threat of All

But not everyone left that meeting in a cheerful, confident spirit.

Felicity herself was deeply worried about something. Her nose seemed to have grown sharper, more beaklike. Her smile had become somehow tighter and quicker to fade. And all the time there'd been a strange uneasy look in those violet-blue eyes.

It didn't show as plainly as it would have on the faces of Ernest Snerdoff and Emily Fitch. *They* never tried to hide their uneasiness. But it was there, all right, on Felicity's as she set out to patrol the building and keep an eye on the Watchdog Squad. Especially on J.G. and others likely to make waves, such as the two youngest Fisher girls.

In fact, her first mission was to steer these three away from the Reference Room and leave Tim Kowalski and Spencer Curtis to watch over things there. They weren't the world's most alert detectives—Spencer, in particular—but at least they were steady and dependable. And, above all, they weren't likely to get on Ms. Fitch's nerves.

Orville's mother, Mrs. Eleanor Grisson, was another who had

problems. She had only just moved into town, and she was already fearing for Orville's health. She was always fussing over him but he now seemed to be in greater danger than ever.

All she'd set out to do that morning was to see her aunt, Gloria Twitchpurse, and quietly enroll the boy as a member of the Junior Library. Hopefully, to get him some good books—clean, brand new ones, free from infectious germs—books that would keep him interested while he got used to his new home and maybe made a few nice, well-behaved friends.

And here he was, dumped in the middle of a war zone with all heck about to be let loose!

"*You're* not getting mixed up in this, Orville!" she muttered. "Let me give that entry form back to Ms. Snell. Right now!"

"Aw, Mom!"

"You know what your nerves are like! I don't want to be sitting up with you having nightmares every night! Your father *would* have something to go to the judge with then!"

"Aw, but . . ." Orville suddenly gave up.

This was his mother's biggest worry. She and his father were having a custody battle over Orville. That was why she'd moved to West Milbury. Out of the way, and hopefully out of reach of her husband's private detectives. They, she knew, were itching to catch her out and prove she was neglecting the kid. In fact, she wasn't sure that one of those photographers *wasn't* a private investigator. He'd been quick enough to snap the boy when it seemed as if Orville was in trouble and looking very distressed!

She caught up with Gloria Twitchpurse on the way out, detaining her at the door. "I have a hairdressing appointment in ten minutes, Aunt, at that place you recommended. And I was wondering . . ."

"Yes, Cuts 'n' Curls," Ms. Twitchpurse broke in. "Mrs. Kowalski's place. She'll take good care of you, Eleanor. That's her son, just going up the stairs. One of Felicity's Watchdog Squad, the quiet fair-haired boy—"

"Yes, yes, Aunt. But it will take two hours, and I don't like leaving Orville that long, especially with all this excitement. As I told you over the phone, his nerves are . . ."

"Yes, Eleanor. I quite understand. Don't worry. I'll have a word with Felicity now. She'll fix him up in a nice quiet corner—out of the way. . . ."

Mary Farrell's worry was not as deep as either Mrs. Grisson's or Felicity's. But it was widespread—all over her body, a tingling uneasiness that made it feel as if her hives were starting up again. She was still seething about her crime scene display.

She'd thought she might have died with anguish back there when the Watchdogs had burst upon the scene. *Her* scene, which she'd worked so hard on and arranged so tastefully!

What with the little Fisher girls tippy-toeing around the carefully chalked outlines and smudging them, and that clown of a brother of hers waving that disgusting old pipe over the body, it was getting to look more like a murder scene from a comic ballet—the sort of ballet they staged at the Drama Club's theater with kids from the local dance academy. A ballet called *Slaughter on West Main Street* or *Mayhem in the Public Library* or something just as dumb!

And to cap it all, some kid had been talking about a performing dog waiting in the wings. She could hear it now, still yapping away in the parking lot!

She was doing some yapping and snapping herself as she went into the lobby with the driver.

"Where d'you think *you're* going?" she said.

He was heading for the front door. His sandy eyelashes blinked nervously. "Back to the store. We're all done here, aren't we?"

"No, we are *not*! We still have the books to select for the Dark Winter Evenings at Home window displays. Mr. Rubinstein fixed it up in return for our help with the contest. Remember?"

The Winter Evenings display was one of Mary's biggest projects. All departments of Rubinstein's were to showcase their latest fall products in settings representing kitchens, bedrooms, game areas, and dens—not forgetting winter fashions and the latest ideas in hobbies and pastimes. Books appropriate to each were to be featured in these backgrounds, just lying around, to show that reading was an important part of the Winter Evenings theme.

And not only were they to be selected by subject matter. Every color coordinator in the store was on Mary's back, hoping she'd pick books with jackets that would match the color of the clothes, shoes, drapes, upholstery, and so on, on display. It would take an awful lot of books and Mary was glad Ms. Twitchpurse had told her to pick out as many as she needed. She'd been glad, too, when Mr. Rubinstein said, "Yes, and take someone to go around the shelves and help carry those you select. Books can get very heavy, and artists like you, Mary, need to be free to concentrate on their work."

But now she wasn't so sure. This *helper* couldn't even remember the job they still had to do!

"Oh, yeah . . . ," he was saying. "I'd nearly forgot. Anyway, I've just got to step out for ten minutes. I'm fresh out of cigarettes."

"Well, don't be any longer!" snapped Mary. "We've got work to do and it won't be easy. Not with all these kids swarming all over the place!"

She groaned and closed her eyes. She was getting one of her headaches.

And now that darned dog was yapping even louder!

Spencer Curtis was another who could still hear the dog. It continued to make *him* very uneasy, too. That's why he was embarking on his Watchdog duties by slowly gorging himself on peanut brittle. He found it soothing while he was chewing and chomping away at it. But, of course, it really made things worse. He knew that, at this rate, there'd soon be none left for Sweets. And that made him feel guilty. And guilty made him miserable. And miserable made him reach for more peanut brittle.

He sighed a deep sugary, buttery sigh.

A guy just couldn't win. . . .

As for Orville, he turned out to be another restless, twitchy worrier like Mary Farrell. He, too, was seething and chafing as his mother and Felicity led him into the Reference Room. In his case, it was because he was itching to join in the quest for clues.

Fat chance of that, he was thinking, with a mother like his fussing over his every move!

Freddie Fisher was the quietest worrier of all. He had overheard Mrs. Grisson talking to Ms. Twitchpurse about Orville, and he was hoping the quiet corner they were fixing up for the kid wouldn't be in the Junior Room.

Orville showed all the signs of being bad news. It was bad enough having to keep an eye out for Benny Stockler, but Orville— no, *thank* you!

Besides, there was something else to keep alert for. A much greater menace than the odd cheat. Freddie was thinking of someone Felicity had mentioned only the evening before—the mysterious personage whose name Felicity didn't even know, whose face she hadn't even seen, whom she'd referred to simply as The Chameleon!

Oh, yes! *That* was what Felicity had been so deeply worried about this morning!

And with very good reason!

10

The Chameleon in the Shadows

Felicity had first broken the news when the Watchdog Squad was helping her plant the clue cards, the evening before the contest.

The library had closed early so that they could get around without disturbing other library users. Also, of course, so that other library users—especially kids—wouldn't be able to see where the cards were being placed. With the light outside just beginning to fade, the deserted rooms had seemed downright spooky.

Freddie thought so anyway, when they were up on the Third Floor, and Felicity was fixing the last of the cards, a golden yellow one, on the door of Mr. Hayes's office.

"You can hardly notice there's a card there at all!" said Tim, as Felicity stood back to inspect her work.

She'd slid the card behind the nameplate, so that its number, *20*, with its key word, *Life*, next to it, couldn't be seen. All that was visible was a thin strip of yellow.

"Practically invisible," said Freddie, bending closer.

"Magic!" murmured Ruth.

"*I* can see it!" said Robyn. "It isn't as shiny as the door."

"It's well camouflaged, anyway," said J.G.

"That's the idea," said Felicity.

"I spotted it!" said Robyn.

"Only because you saw it being put there!" said Ruth.

"Yeah," said Julie. "So shut up. And don't go blabbing about it tomorrow. It's a secret."

J.G. sighed. He turned to Felicity to show that he for one was way above this kind of foolish kids' prattle. "Is that why you've called it the 'hardest clue of all,' Felicity?" He plucked a copy of the entry form from the pile they'd been photocopying, ready for tomorrow.

"Yes!" said Ruth. "But I bet this is what you mean by going 'right to the top,' Felicity." She pointed to the list headed "Clues About Clues." "It means going to *Mr. Hayes's* door. The top librarian's. Right?"

"Keep your voice down," Felicity murmured. "Yes."

"You did the same thing down in the Junior Room, didn't you, Felicity?" said J.G., "when you put a gold card in among all those yellow black-eyed Susans."

"Sure," said Felicity. "And red cards were placed where there was red in the background. Like the back of the almanac the murder victim's going to be clutching—as if a scrap of the red binding had come loose."

"It's really a kind of camouflage, isn't it?" said J.G. "That's one neat idea!"

Felicity shrugged. "Oh, I don't know. It's an old trick. Thieves use it all the time. When I was working for Coast-to-Coast Investigations, I once had to track down someone who'd been stealing valuable birds from a pheasant farm in the dead of winter. We'd all seen his footprints in the snow, but never a glimpse of *him*."

Spencer Curtis looked up. "Like the Invisible Man?" He became suddenly decisive. "My dog Sweets would've sniffed him out!"

J.G. sneered. "Yeah! If the guy had been eating something like popcorn coated with molasses . . ."

"Anyway," said Felicity, "when I finally caught up with him, we found out his secret. And yes, I can see you've guessed it, John. He was dressed all in white—white parka, white ski pants, white gloves, even white boots. Nearly invisible against the snow."

"Camouflaged," murmured Ruth thoughtfully. She liked to practice new words. "Camouflaged, camouflaged, camouflaged."

"All right, already!" said J.G. "There's no need for—"

Felicity stepped in again. "It was the bloodstains that gave him away in the end," she said softly.

If she'd barked it out in the voice of Ernest Snerdoff, she couldn't have gotten their attention more speedily.

"Bl— *what* bloodstains, Felicity?" faltered Ruth.

"His *own* blood, Felicity?" said J.G. "You . . . you shot him?"

"No. It was blood from a pheasant whose throat he'd slit to stop it from squawking and raising the alarm. It sure ruined *that* thief's camouflage!"

Holly Jenks spoke up. "And you say thieves use camouflage a lot, Felicity?"

"Yes. Sneak thieves especially. You'd be surprised at the lengths some of them go to to melt into the background. I once collared a notorious thief who stole from cars. A woman. *She* used to dress like a meter maid and . . ."

Felicity broke off. Her nose took on that beaky look. Her mouth became tight.

She was mad at herself.

She could have kicked herself black and blue.

She'd noticed the look on Freddie's face—his uneasiness—and also a similarly distressed look on Ruth's and the other two Fisher girls'.

Their father, Felicity remembered, had been a car thief, himself. Stealing *from* cars, mainly. He'd even been jailed for it—to the great shame and distress of his family. Especially Freddie.

She quickly changed the subject.

"Anyway, about these clues. I guess I've been taking a leaf out of The Chameleon's book!"

The strange name made them stare. It was the way Felicity had said it, too. Like it was very special. With a capital *T* and a capital *C*.

Felicity, in her embarrassment, had given it all she'd got.

"Chameleon, Felicity? Isn't that an animal?" said Tim.

"Or a flower?" said Julie.

"A reptile, actually," said Ruth.

They were all sounding relieved at this change of subject.

"A kind of lizard," Ruth went on, gathering enthusiasm. "Its skin changes color according to what it's standing against. Leaves, it turns green. Bark, it turns brown. It makes it very hard to spot."

"Yes, Felicity," said Holly. "It even shows the outlines of things. Like twigs, or . . . or bricks on a wall that it's climbing up, doesn't it?"

This was too much for J.G. "She's thinking of a chameleon she's seen in a Loonytoon cartoon!" he sneered. "Bricks on a wall! Huh!"

"I am *not* then!" cried Holly. "And you pronounce it *Kameleon*, like it begins with a *K*, not *Sham*eleon!"

"Whatever!" said J.G. airily. "It *is* a sham, anyway. That's its M.O."

When he used that tone, J.G. not only got his opponent mad, he got everyone mad.

"What do *you* know about it!" jeered Ruth.

And that was when the door burst open and Mr. Hayes appeared.

"*Hey, hey, hey*! Hold the noise down, kids. I'm trying to work in here and . . . Oh, hello, Felicity!"

"Yes, come on, you guys," she said, after apologizing for them. "We have more work to do ourselves. And there's something very special I'd better tell you. About the sneak thief *I* call The Chameleon . . . Let's go down to Club headquarters and we'll discuss it there."

Any excuse to use the old library van was good enough for them. Especially in the fading light, when the shadows were deepening, and the street lights were shining brighter, throwing more and more shadows by the minute. But with this promise of further information about what sounded very sinister, Felicity's invitation was irresistible

But before they could move away, Mr. Hayes said, "Oh, there's no need for that, Felicity. So long as they keep their voices down—"

"That's okay, Mr. Hayes, we're all done in here anyway." Felicity gave him a wry smile. "And after what I have to tell them, they won't be able to keep their voices down! I've decided to put them on red alert for The Chameleon, after all." Mr. Hayes frowned.

"Oh? You sure that's wise, Felicity? I mean what they don't know can't hurt them and . . ."

Mr. Hayes was wrong there. He seemed to realize this as he looked down on the eight young faces turned up to him. Every muscle on every face was under obvious strain as eyes widened, mouths gaped, and ears (yes, he could swear he saw it happening!), ears actually pricked up!

They all seemed vastly relieved, anyway, when Felicity spoke.

"After the fax I received today, Mr. Hayes, there's nothing else I *can* do, I'm afraid. It's what they don't know that *could* hurt them! The information I'm talking about is on what they used to call, in the private investigation business, a *need-to-know* basis."

That last remark sent another electric thrill through the kids. Especially their leader. J.G. was already moving to the top of the stairs.

"You heard her, you guys," he said, his gray eye piercing the shadows down below, as if he suspected The Chameleon was lurking there already. "Let's go!"

11

A Message from the Chameleon

In the few weeks since the Junior Mystery Club had taken it over, the old mobile library van had been given a new look.

Some of the book stacks had been moved to the sides. This created more space down the middle, making room for some small tables and chairs. Some of the shelves had been removed, too, to create spaces for taller objects. Objects like several bulletin boards, propped up at intervals along the length of the van, each displaying one of Freddie's trial designs for the Watchdogs' name tags.

As soon as he'd suggested adding the eyes the kids had been all for it. And when J.G. then went on to personalize his own tag by coloring the eyes, most of the Watchdogs had clamored for personalized tags of their own.

Unfortunately, none of *them* had odd-colored eyes that could be fixed so easily. But they all had ideas, and Freddie had his work cut out that afternoon, following their instructions.

So, as soon as Felicity switched on the lights, Freddie's artwork stared out from the various alcoves along both sides. It was as if the kids had just come into the light of a campfire and were surrounded by hungry wolves.

Holly Jenks had insisted on the lashes because she was a plump, plain girl and nobody ever complimented her except her grand-mother, who'd once said she had "very nice eyes." Holly had also asked for the contest banner to be shown, because it helped to prettify the dog image, like a hair ribbon.

For Ruth, Freddie had tried to convey her glasses. Then he'd realized the pointed ears gave the logo an added owl-like look, suiting Ruth to a T. Then she'd said if Holly's logo showed the banner, *she* wanted it, too. So he'd added it to hers and thrown in the poles at the top of the peaks, making the design even more owl-like, as if it had tufted ears.

Spencer's was very simple. All he wanted was for "the eyes to look like true, genuine beagle's," even if it had to have wolf's ears. So Freddie had copied "true, genuine beagle's eyes" from a snapshot of Sweets that Spencer carried with him everywhere—itself getting very dog-eared and sticky with constant handling.

Julie's was also easy, just so long as he made *her* eyelashes "longer and curlier" than Holly's. But it was Robyn who gave him the most grief. She had insisted on adding the question marks that Felicity had said were to be dangling down the front of the building on white cards. Robyn had liked that. She was always being told off for asking too many questions.

Well, *she* saw it as part of a Watchdog's job to do just that. To challenge anyone she saw acting suspiciously.

"What are you doing that for?"

Or "Why don't you put it back where it was?"

Or "Didn't you hear what Felicity said?"

Or even "Are you dumb or what?"

The only tags that hadn't given Freddie any trouble were his own and Tim's. All *they* wanted was the simple basic design, clear and businesslike.

Other objects that had found homes in the extra tall shelf spaces included a desktop copying machine, on loan from Mr. Hayes's office; a fourteen-inch TV with a VCR, donated by Felicity; and a small blackboard, on which Mary Farrell had sketched out a rough picture of how the front of the library was going to look with the banners and dangling cards.

On the remaining shelves, a collection of books had started to build up again. Not the regular mix of subjects—fact and fiction—but only the books that happened to have some link to a particular case or project.

There was a manual about footprints, for example. And another about simple disguises, called *New ID's in the Blink of an Eye: Twenty Quick Tips for Amateur Actors and Others.*

These practical working books were still lying flat on the shelves, littered about among other objects such as magnifying glasses (in three different sizes), folded street maps of West Milbury and nearby towns, packets of typing paper, a tub filled with pencils and ballpoint pens, several boxes of coloring pencils, and a bunch of colored cards. These last were mostly in calling-card sizes, like those to be used for the contest, but some had been cut down into various smaller sizes, with which Felicity had been experimenting.

This was no mere overflow library extension. This was a real workshop for young detectives!

No one entering the van that evening had paid much attention to any of the objects on the shelves. And no one noticed a new addition—a volume bound in red with gilt lettering that Felicity reached for as soon as she got in.

But when Felicity sat down at one of the tables and pulled out a large envelope, their attention was riveted. J.G., who had made straight for his favorite perch, high above the others, on the back of the driver's seat, quickly jumped down and dragged a chair next to Felicity's. Soon they were all crowding around to get a closer look at the sheet of paper she was taking from the envelope.

"First, you'd better take a look at *this*!" she said. "It's a photocopy of the message The Chameleon left last week, addressed to me, just after the contest was first announced. The original looks even creepier."

A buzz went up—a mixture of murmured, mystified "Hey!"s and awed "Wow!"s—as they clustered closer. Even J.G. hadn't any clearer comment to make as he gaped at that weird message:

"Stop thief! Stop thief!" There is a magic in the sound. The tradesman leaves his counter, and the carman his waggon; the butcher throws down his tray; the baker his basket; the milk-man his pail; the errand-boy his parcels; the school-boy his marbles; the paviour his pickaxe; the child his battledore. Away they run, pell-mell, helter-skelter, slap-dash: tearing, yelling, and screaming: knocking down the passengers as they turn the corners: rousing up the dogs, and astonishing the fowls; and streets, squares, and courts, re-echo with the sound.

"Stop thief! Stop thief!" The cry is taken up by a hundred voices, and the crowd accumulate at every turning. Away they fly, splashing through the mud, and rattling along the pavements: up go the windows, out run the people, onward bear the mob, a whole audience desert Punch in the very thickest of the plot, and, joining the rushing throng, swell the shout, and lend fresh vigour to the cry, "Stop thief! Stop thief!"

"Stop thief! Stop thief!" There is a passion *for hunting something* deeply implanted in the human breast. One wretched, breathless child, panting with exhaustion; terror in his looks; agony in his eye; large drops of perspiration streaming down his face, strains every nerve to make head upon his pursuers; and as they follow on his track, and gain upon him every instant, they hail his decreasing strength with still louder shout, and whoop and scream with joy. "Stop thief!" Ay, stop him for God's sake, were it only in

mercy! Stopped at last! A clever blow. He is down upon the pavement; and the crowd eagerly gather round him : each new comer, jostling and struggling with the others to catch a glimpse. "Stand aside!" "Give him a little air!" "Nonsense! he don't deserve it." "Where's the gentleman?" "Here he is, coming down the street." "Make room there for the gentleman!" "Is this the boy, sir!" "Yes."

Oliver lay, covered with mud and dust, and bleeding from the mouth, looking wildly round upon the heap of faces that surrounded him, when the old gentleman was officiously dragged and pushed into the circle by the foremost of the pursuers.

"Yes," said the gentleman, "I am afraid it is the boy."

Some of them couldn't make it out at all.

"What is it?" whispered Holly.

"That's The Chameleon's message," said Felicity, slowly tracing the words with the tip of a finger.

Ruth read them out in a hushed voice. " 'I'll be back'?" She looked up at Felicity. "What's he mean?"

"He or she, The Chameleon, means exactly what it says there, I'm afraid."

"But it isn't *signed*," wailed Holly. "It doesn't *say* The Chameleon!"

"It doesn't need to," said Felicity. "The stuck-on words have been cut from the same book, so that they seem part of the background."

"C-chameleon writing!" stammered Holly.

"Exactly!" said Felicity. "Isn't that just the kind of message chameleons would write—if they *could* write?"

The buzz arose again, more "wow"s than "hey"s this time. It was beginning to look as if they were dealing with a huge lizard thing with human intelligence! A monster that could understand, and use, human speech!

"Jurassic Park never had nothing like this!" said Spencer in an awed whisper, casting an anxious glance at the darkening windows.

This caused Robyn to huddle up closer to Ruth and whisper, "I . . . I'm *frightened*, Ruthie!"

"But it *has* been written by a real person," Felicity was quick to point out. "Or cut out and stuck on by one."

J.G. came out of his daze. "Cut out from *where*, Felicity?"

"From *this*." Felicity touched the red volume.

Ruth gasped. She'd already taken a good look at the gold

lettering and wondered what *Oliver Twist*, by Charles Dickens, was doing there.

After all, she had read *Oliver Twist*. She'd first seen it as a movie on TV and told Felicity about it, and Felicity had had Elaine take her into the Adult Department and show her which shelf it was on. And that was what was puzzling Ruth now.

Oliver Twist was about a horrible old man, a criminal, who ran a special school for young pickpockets. Well, if anyone was running a special school for kids in *here*, it was Felicity herself. And she was no horrible old criminal! She was the exact opposite! An ex-private investigator who was young and pretty and kind, running a sort of school for wannabe detectives.

Felicity was an expert at reading people's thoughts from their expressions and eye movements. "Yes, Ruth," she said. "You probably borrowed this very volume and read this very page." She sighed and turned to where that page had been, before being brutally ripped out. *"Page seventy-one.* The cutout words were from pages seventy-three or seventy-four." She turned to the gap in the book where they'd been. "See the ragged edges *there*, too?"

Ruth was seeing them only as a wavy blur. There were tears in her eyes as she gazed at the damage. She'd *enjoyed* that book! Her first from the grown-up library, too!

"So whatever else this person has done," said Felicity, looking almost as sad as Ruth, "or is *intending* to do, he or she has ruined a fine old volume and spoiled the set."

There was an angry growl.

Damage to books was Holly's speciality. In the past, she'd spent hours tracking down books that had been scribbled on or torn by their borrowers' baby brothers or sisters. Some kids said that made her a fink, but her skill at tracking down the culprits is what had first attracted Felicity's attention. Even J.G. had been impressed—enough to let her join his group when they were helping Felicity solve the Purloined Corn Popper Mystery.

But right now, Holly was really mad. The kids' scribbles had been innocent. But this was deliberate. Perpetrated by some grown-up person, not some two-year-old!

"Well he—or she—is a dirty low-down vandal!" she said. "That's what *I* think!"

Felicity sighed again. "That's the least of the damage this person has caused!" she said softly.

There was another growl. Not as loud as Holly's. More of a groan, really.

J.G. was looking at Holly as if he wondered what he'd ever seen in her as a junior detective. Detectives should be tough and cool at all times, he was thinking. Like him. They should never, ever, have tears in their eyes. Whether of sadness, like Ruth Fisher's, or rage, like Holly Jenks's.

He got to his feet abruptly and pulled out the old pipe. "Can't you trace who borrowed it last, Felicity?" He used the pipe stem to turn back to the date-stamp page of the vandalized volume.

Felicity shook her head. "It wasn't borrowed in the regular way. The perpetrator simply sneaked it from the shelves without getting it checked out."

"Didn't anyone see anyone acting suspiciously?"

"I guess not," said Felicity. "The Chameleon would make sure of *that*. This is one clever person—as we at this library know to our cost."

J.G.'s eyebrows shot up even higher. "He—or she—has struck before, then?"

"Several times," said Felicity grimly.

J.G. then came out with the sixty-four-thousand-dollar question: "Just *when* before, Felicity? And why doesn't anyone know whether it's a he or she by now?"

12

The Chameleon's M.O.

Before Felicity could reply, they heard the sound of a car's engine, getting louder. The glare of its headlights swept across the Watchdogs' headquarters. Even the Watchdog logos seemed to stare out in alarm from their niches and shrink as the glare swept by.

After that, silence for a few seconds. Then the slam of a car's door, two slams, but no footsteps. Whoever had gotten out was just standing there, looking around or up at the twilit sky, maybe for the evening star or the young moon.

"I'll bet it's someone who didn't know the library was closing early," said Felicity.

"I'll take a look," said J.G. He sprang to the windows, cupped his hands, and peered out into the gathering dark.

"Anything?" said Tim.

"Huh-uh!" grunted J.G., moving on fast to try further along, and knocking over one of the bulletin boards.

"Hey . . . watch it!" snapped Freddie.

"Station wagon," murmured J.G., still peering through cupped hands. "There's a man and woman. . . . It looks like Mary and one of her boyfriends and . . . uh . . . yeah . . . that's who it is."

He sounded as if he'd suddenly lost interest.

Felicity said, "Probably she's come for a last look at the building before it gets its banners and hanging cards tomorrow morning.

She said she'd be bringing them herself, along with the scene-of-the-crime stuff."

J.G. sighed. *"That's* our Mary! When she has a job like this, she has to check everything first. We've known her to prowl around outside Rubinstein's windows until midnight if she has a big display the next day. Sometimes, you'd think she was planning a major bank robbery!"

Felicity's worried frown had come back. "Anyway," she said. "About The Chameleon . . ."

"Yes, *ma'am*!" J.G. nearly fell over himself in his haste to resume his seat.

"All I know so far is what has been deduced from the details of those earlier crimes and especially the method," said Felicity. "That's usually where a good detective finds the best clues to what the criminal is like and what he or she's likely to do next. Sometimes the *only* clues."

Completely hooked now, J.G. said, "What clues *did* you find, Felicity? Pay close attention, you guys!"

"Well," said Felicity, "this really takes us back to the questions you were asking before the car came. Why does no one know yet whether The Chameleon's a man or woman? Answer: Because no one has seen the person. Not *knowingly*. It could be anyone. A borrower or even a member of the staff. A stranger or someone we see every day. An adult or some really smart kid."

They began to look at one another rather furtively.

"A chameleon, though!" insisted Robyn. "We do know *that*, don't we, Felicity?"

She spoke as if the perpetrator went about in a lizard suit. And that was how most of the younger ones were thinking by now. A lizard suit that changed color according to the room the wearer went into. Bright green for the Junior Room itself, where the walls had recently been repainted a cheerful pale lime shade, and a dull light brown for the Reference Room.

But J.G. was already pursuing his own line of questioning. "You said he—or she—has struck before *several times*? Causing big trouble?"

"Oh yes," said Felicity. "I can tell it's the same person because of the Chameleon-type M.O. And when I said several times before, I mean before I started work here, a few months ago."

"Nothing's ever happened since?" persisted J.G.

"No. Not *yet*."

"I bet he doesn't *dare* with you around, Felicity!" said Ruth.

Felicity smiled sadly. "Thanks, Ruth. But I think this person is saving up the worst just for me. That's why this message was sent. Mocking me."

J.G. pressed on. "But these other times . . . ?"

"I got to know about them from Mr. Hayes. I was very interested, of course."

"Of course . . . ," murmured J.G., as one great detective to another.

"When felonies start happening in the same unusual way more than once or twice, you get to thinking there's a serial criminal at work. In this case, a serial sneak thief. In fact, that's how I've been used to thinking of this person. The Serial Sneak Thief. Until I got this message. Now it's just The Chameleon."

"And causing big trouble, huh?" murmured J.G. "Like what big trouble, Felicity?" His gray eye was looking very steely, very silvery.

"Just before I came. Up in the Natural History Museum Pets Corner."

"Oh, the ferret!" chimed several voices.

"Yes."

"Was *that* The Chameleon?" said Ruth.

"No. The ferret," said Julie. "Benny Stockler's ferret, when it got loose. Killed some rabbits. Nearly broke their owners' hearts. Don't you remember *that*? It even bit Mr. Peters's finger when he tried to catch it."

"Correct," said Felicity. "But who do you think freed the ferret, Julie?"

"The . . . The Chameleon?"

"That's what I think now," said Felicity. "I've been asking around. Benny swears that Matilda's collar had been loosened. At least one notch. And some kind of grease had been smeared all around the inside. And the trouble could have been much worse!" she added angrily.

"Yes! Mr. Peters could have gotten rabies!" said Holly.

"No, Holly," said Felicity. "Matilda had had all her shots. But I was thinking there could have been several nasty accidents. I understand there was some panicking and some little kids could have been trampled in the rush."

"Reckless endangerment!" said J.G.

"The jerk!" Robyn burst out, picturing herself as one of the victims. "The dirty rotten . . . !"

"Easy, Robyn," murmured Ruth.

"Then there was the time when Elizabeth Christopher—" Felicity began.

"The TV soap star!" said Holly. "Yes!"

"—came to launch the publication of her new book at a party in the Adult Department—"

"Packed with people who'd come to get her autograph," said Holly, getting excited. "Mostly women. My mother—"

"Let Felicity tell it!" J.G. ordered sternly. "I think I know what's coming. The white rats. Right, Felicity?"

"Yes," said Felicity. "Half a dozen of them. Brought along in someone's pockets and let loose in there. It wasn't Benny this time, or some other kid being mischievous. My own theory is that whoever did it went on to take advantage of the confusion and steal the star's twenty-thousand-dollar coat, which she'd left in Mr. Hayes's office for . . . uh . . . safekeeping."

"Well, if he tries white rats again—" Spencer began.

Freddie cut in. "Wasn't something else stolen from Mr. Hayes's office at the time of the ferret, Felicity?"

"Yes. Gold and silver trophies. Awards for the best small-town library in the Northeast. *Very* valuable, especially to Mr. Hayes and the rest of the staff. Even Mr. Snerdoff's Best Kept Lobby award was stolen, too." She shook her head. "And this is what I mean about The Chameleon's M.O. He waits until there's a special attraction, bringing in lots of people. Next, he does something to cause a disturbance. Then he strikes, when nobody is likely to see him with all the fuss going on. . . ."

"You're saying *he* now," Julie broke in. "And *him*."

"Yes, well it still could be *she* and *her*," said Felicity. "We just don't know. Uh . . . what were you going to say, Spencer? About if The Chameleon tries white rats again?"

"Yes, Felicity. I could bring Sweets in to patrol the building and pounce the minute they're loosed!"

"He's a dog, not a cat!" said Ruth.

"He isn't a bad ratter, either!" said Spencer. "He'd be onto 'em in a flash!"

Holly shuddered, thinking of the way Sweets dealt with a rat during their investigation into the Corn Popper Mystery.

"If they were *candy* rats," sneered J.G., "maybe there'd be some sense. . . ."

"Or *molasses* rats," Holly cut in.

"Anyway," said Felicity, "I doubt if The Chameleon will try the same thing twice. A thief like that knows how to vary it. But there were other more concrete clues."

"Such as?" J.G.'s gray eye was glittering again.

"Well, as I said, no one noticed anyone taking these things from the building, and that was very strange." Felicity spoke slowly, as if trying to visualize the smallest details. "The trophies would have had to be removed in something like a suitcase or a sack. And *they* would have been too bulky to have gone unnoticed." She looked around at the eight eager but baffled faces. "So how did the thief get them out of the building?"

13

Felicity Sketches a Solid Clue

Freddie was the first to suggest an answer, beating even J.G. to it.

"Hid them somewhere in the building. And took them out later, when the heat was off. Maybe *days* later."

"That's an old shoplifter's trick," said Felicity.

"Yeah!" said J.G.

"Usually it fails," said Felicity. "Store detectives always make a search for valuable articles that might have been stashed like that. If I'd been working here, I'd certainly have done that."

"Sure," said J.G. "There'd be nothing smart about The Chameleon pulling *that* penny-ante trick!"

"Well what would *you* have done then?" said Freddie.

"Yeah!" said Ruth.

J.G. gave them his snootiest look. "How would I know? *I'm* not a thief. I'm a detective."

Felicity stepped in quickly. "You might know more if there'd been some solid clue." She reached for a sketching block and began to draw. "Like the one I found out about later."

"What was that, Felicity?" asked Tim.

"It turned up right here, under this van." She held up the sketch.

"A cardboard box, just right for removing the trophies stolen that day."

She scribbled in a few measurements, plus what looked like a bunch of snails or spiders, clinging to the sides.

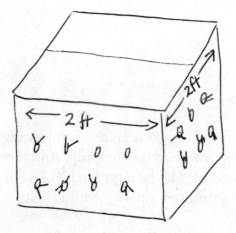

"Well didn't anyone spot something that big being taken out?" said J.G. "I bet *I* would have!"

"Someone *might* have," said Felicity. "But without realizing what it contained. Other than the straw, of course."

"Straw, Felicity?" said Holly.

"Yes. The straw was still there when Mr. Snerdoff spotted it under this vehicle. It also had these holes punched in it."

Felicity indicated what some had mistaken for spiders.

"Oh, yes!" said Julie. "With bits of straw poking out!"

"Mr. Snerdoff, huh?" murmured J.G. Like the gun-jumper he was, he'd pounced on the first name mentioned.

Felicity put him right. "Oh, *he* only happened to find the box when he was making his litter roundup in the parking lot."

Tim had been considering the details. "Hey, yeah! I think I can see what happened!"

"So do I!" said Ruth. "It was dumped by a Pet Club member. Something that had carried a rabbit, maybe. Maybe one of the rabbits killed by the ferret."

"On the way *in*, it probably did," said Felicity. "In among the straw were a few lettuce leaves, brown and shriveled by the time the box was found. But on the day of the Pet Club fiasco, they would still have been fresh."

She picked up the sketch pad again. "Also in there, they found Elaine's gloves and hat. They were stolen, too. Inexpensive imitation fur ones. Elaine doesn't hold with the use of real fur."

"But I didn't know *they'd* been stolen!" said Ruth.

"You wouldn't. At the time, everyone was more concerned about the trophies," said Felicity. "Or those poor rabbits. Even Elaine hadn't been upset much about *her* things. She said it served her right, anyway. She shouldn't have left them lying around."

"Yes, I remember now," said Holly. "She even joked about it. Said maybe that vicious ferret had made off with them. Dragged them away, thinking they were some more tasty, furry creatures."

"Instead of which, that vicious Chameleon had stolen them," said Felicity.

J.G. looked up sharply. "Oh?"

"Yes," said Felicity. "As I said, they were found with the straw in the box. Everyone thought that whoever had taken them had realized they weren't worth more than a few dollars and dumped them in disgust. But The Chameleon doesn't make mistakes like that. They'd been stolen deliberately, for disguise purposes."

"But if he'd gone out wearing them, he'd have been spotted straight away," said J.G. "Even if they fit him."

"Not if the Chameleon is a woman," said Holly. "A *woman* wouldn't have looked peculiar wearing them."

"Him or her," said Felicity, "one thing's for sure. They wouldn't be for *wearing*."

"But you said they'd be part of The Chameleon's *disguise*!" said J.G.

"They were. But the *box's* disguise, not the person's. With the air holes and straw and lettuce, anyone asking to see inside that box on the way out would take one look at the bundles of fur nestling there in the straw and would think they were just pets. A mother rabbit and two young ones, maybe. When all the time the straw was concealing stolen trophies!"

They stared at her.

"There was even a bunch of holes in the *bottom*," Felicity went on.

"More air holes?" whispered Robyn.

"No, honey. *Finger* holes."

"Huh?" Even J.G. looked baffled.

"Yes," said Felicity. "For the thief to put his fingers through. The fingers of the hand supporting the box from underneath. In case of being stopped on the way out. Then he or she could wiggle the gloves through the straw so they'd look like real living creatures."

"Eek!" Holly squealed at the very thought.

"Wow!" gasped J.G. with a faint grudging grin. "You've got to hand it to this . . . this Chameleon!"

"The only thing that's got to be handed to The Chameleon," said Felicity, "is a good stiff jail sentence before that person does something really terrible!"

"Amen to that!" said Holly.

"Anyway, having figured out the way The Chameleon operated that time, I think I can now see how the valuable coat was spirited out of the building," Felicity said.

"Wearing it?" said Spencer.

Felicity shook her head. "I doubt, even if The Chameleon had been a woman, she could have gotten away with *wearing* it. Ms. Christopher is unusually tall and very slim. Six foot and only just over one-hundred-and-twenty pounds. She used to be a top model before becoming a TV star. In fact, her nickname at school was Skinny Liz."

"The title of her new book!" said Holly. "My mother had it autographed! She said it was worth getting her tights ruined in the rush after the white rats were loosed."

J.G. waved his pipe airily. "Now we've heard the fashion news, would you mind letting Felicity tell us about how the coat happened to be spirited out of the building?"

"It was a *vicuna* coat," Holly said. "Like camel hair but much more expensive. The most expensive there is. It's made from—"

"I don't care if it's made of spun gold!" said J.G. "How'd it get out so no one would notice, Felicity? Did The Chameleon simply carry it?"

"No. It was worn all right!"

"But you said . . ."

"The *mirror* wore it," Felicity said. "The Chameleon carried the mirror. That's my theory, anyway."

J.G. frowned, completely fazed. So were the others.

"What mirror, Felicity?" said Ruth.

"Another inexpensive article stolen that day. And like Elaine's hat and gloves, no one took it into account. Just a cheap, flimsy, full-length mirror they use in fashion and menswear stores everywhere. Mr. Hayes bought one in honor of Ms. Christopher's visit, to prop up in his office for her convenience when using it as a powder room. All The Chameleon did was wrap the coat roughly around the mirror and tie it with coarse string. The way moving men do with more expensive mirrors and much cheaper coats, so the mirrors don't get cracked. And it would be carried out that way. Just another moving person taking care of a customer's mirror."

Holly gasped. "At twenty-thousand dollars a throw!"

"Anyway," said Felicity, "now that we know something about the way The Chameleon operates, we can deduce something about what that person might be like, can't we?"

"Yeah!" said Tim Kowalski. "Someone who doesn't care who gets hurt."

"Unscrupulous!" said Ruth.

"Mean and nasty and horrible!" said Robyn.

"Reckless and dangerous," said J.G.

"Someone who knows his or her way around the library," said Freddie thoughtfully.

"Someone very clever at blending into the background," said Holly.

"Yeah, yeah! Like a chameleon!" said J.G. "We *know* that!"

"Someone good at *improvising*!" said Julie.

The others stared at her.

"You *know*," said Julie. "Like Madame Zelda is always telling us at Tap and Ballet. Quick at grabbing any opportunity or article that might be useful to him or her in their performance."

"The Chameleon goes around *stealing*!" growled J.G. "Not *dancing*."

"I know what you mean, Julie," said Felicity. "And you're right. . . . So now let's see what the *profiler* has to say about this person."

She was removing another sheet of paper from the envelope.

J.G. went to the back of her chair to get a better look.

"A profiler?" said Holly.

"Yes," said Felicity. "He studies reports about crimes committed by unknown perpetrators. He can work out, from the details of a crime, various things about the criminal. His or her age, occupation, habits, preferences, and so on.

"The one who wrote *this* profile is one of the best. Professor Ames, used regularly by my old firm, Coast-to-Coast Investigations. He also does work for the FBI, mainly on murder cases. He specializes in serial killers. . . ."

14

A Very Scary Report

J.G. had been prepared to read the lines of close-spaced typing, but even before he'd focused on the words, his eyes had shot wide open again. The page was a riot of color—yellow shafts of highlighting, red stars, black arrows, and troops of dancing exclamation marks.

The report must have been *very* disturbing.

But Felicity began reading out its findings in a calm enough voice. She held the pages of the report at an angle in front of her, so that most of the kids saw only the back of those pages. She'd also laid down flat on the table an enlarged copy of The Chameleon's message so they could all take another, closer look at it.

For the first few minutes J.G. contented himself just with listening to what Felicity was saying. He'd meant to press on ahead and read that report for himself over her shoulder.

But right now he was still reeling with the shock of seeing Felicity's doodles.

"'The person who sent this message,'" she began, reading from Professor Ames's report, "'certainly knows his way around the works of Charles Dickens.'"

"Yes!" Ruth chimed in. "With a pair of scissors!"

"'This is clearly evident from his choice of the page from *Oliver Twist*.'"

All heads bent closer to the photocopy.

" 'Note the fact that it starts with the cry of "Stop thief! Stop thief!" ' "

They all nodded.

Felicity then continued to read out the profiler's report.

" 'And "Stop thief!" is repeated *twice* in the second paragraph, and yet again at the beginning of the third paragraph.' "

Felicity looked up again. "And that makes it eight times in all," she said. "Nine, really, because the word *I* in *I'll* has been stuck over the top of another 'Stop thief!' I must admit I hadn't spotted it myself, not *so* many times."

"I . . . ," began J.G. He was going to say "*I* did, Felicity!" but then realized he'd be lying. "Go on, Felicity," he murmured. "What does he say next?"

" 'What the sender of the message is really doing is getting Charles Dickens to state his underlying message for him. A message that is really a boast, saying, "I'm a thief, but you won't stop *me*! Nobody will stop *me*!" ' "

J.G. had now caught up with that very passage. Felicity had illuminated it with a thick band of yellow highlight and scribbled a border of red asterisks all around it.

"Well, we'll see about *that*," he said grimly.

Other murmurs were rising.

"Yeah!"

"You bet we will!"

"If he tries anything tomorrow . . ."

"Don't worry, Felicity! Us Watchdogs will take care of *that*!"

"Especially if Sweets gets his chance to join in!"

Felicity smiled wanly. "Thanks. But let me continue with Professor Ames's report. We'll need to know about what kind of person we should be keeping a look-out for . . . and now the report gets down to the nitty-gritty.

"Because of The Chameleon's knowledge of Dickens, Professor Ames thinks we could be looking at the work of someone with a diploma or degree in English Literature. Someone who could be a teacher, or a writer or author himself, or even a *librarian*."

"A . . . a *librarian*, Felicity?"

"I'm afraid so, Ruth. But listen. The profiler goes on to say this: 'His knowledge of the library, its rooms and routines, certainly suggests an employee or ex-employee. . . . I'd go for *ex*-employee myself,' he adds, 'because the persistent nature of the thefts suggests someone with a grudge.'"

J.G. had lost his place again, there were so many highlights and red stars and screaming exclamation points at this stage.

"'Or someone who'd once been turned down for a job at the library,'" Felicity was reading on. "'Maybe Mr. Hayes is the real target. Or, of course, it could be some smart kid with a grudge.'"

"*I* don't have any grudge!" J.G. burst out.

Felicity smiled and shook her head. "No, John! The profiler goes straight on to say, 'But I don't think so. He'd have to be a smarter kid than any *I've* known, to dream up things like this. But if . . .'"

Felicity brought her reading to a close here. She looked up.

"He then goes on to give us a general caution, saying The Chameleon could be rather dangerous."

"Well, we knew that already," said Tim.

"Yes. Dangerous to pet rabbits and people's tights!" said Holly.

"And valuable volumes!" said Ruth.

"And little kids!" said Robyn.

But J.G. knew better. His eyes were sharply focused by now on what Professor Ames had actually written. And it was this:

"But if it *is* an adult, then watch out, Felicity! He could be extremely dangerous, especially if anyone gets in the way of one of his capers, *of which I am sure he is insanely proud.*"

86

That was almost the end of the report. J.G. could see why Felicity hadn't read it aloud and so risked giving some of the younger kids nightmares.

And the last passage of all was even scarier. It was surrounded by red tongues of flame doodled by Felicity. Like this:

> But the message itself is what bothers me the most. In fact, in my career as a profiler for the FBI I have only seen one other example of a criminal using a printed page to convey a message cut out and compiled from another page from the same book, chameleonwise. That was a note sent to the police by a serial murderer about his next strike!

15

Cheats

During the first hour that Saturday morning the contest made peaceful progress.

Sure, at the very start, many kids acted as if it were a race. They'd take a quick look around and pounce on any gleam of yellow or flash of red that happened to catch their eye. Smarter kids were more crafty. They'd begin by hanging around, pretending to read one of the books, but noting where the sharp-eyed pounced. Then when no one seemed to be observing them, they'd reach out and, without removing the clue card, ju-u-st slip it into plainer view, bend back its corner, and glance sideways at the number and word marked there. Since most cards bore only a single number and single short word, both could be held in mind for several seconds and noted down well away from the card itself, without giving away its location.

Even the more impatient contestants soon got wise to the advantages of this quiet, pussyfooting approach.

So no innocent borrowers were elbowed out of the way or otherwise disturbed in the Adult Department or, more importantly, in the Reference Room. No complaints were made to the staff. Few attempts at outright cheating were made.

Soon, Felicity's anxious frown began to clear.

There seemed to be hardly any need for the Watchdog Squad, after all. Not as far as the *contestants* were concerned, anyway.

The only really blatant cheating attempts occurred when some kids tried to enlist the Watchdogs' help.

As when one of the older boys approached Holly Jenks in the Junior Room.

Beginning by telling her he admired her shirt, he quickly went on to talk about the clue cards.

"Naturally, *you* know where they're hidden, right?"

"Naturally!" was Holly's reply. "But I'm not telling *you*!"

"No, but you *could* say whether I'm getting warmer or colder. Huh?"

"*Could* but *won't*!" said Holly, firmly.

The wise guy then switched to bribery, saying he'd share his M & M's with her if she'd cooperate. She still refused, so he upped the ante to one whole Hershey bar.

Holly loved chocolate. But she told the tempter to get lost. Her mouth was watering, and it came out as "Get losht!"

This encouraged him into thinking he was in with a chance, and he raised his offer to "One complete bar now, plus a half for each word you direct me to."

In the end, she told him he couldn't bribe *her*.

"Not for all the chocolate in Hersheyville!" she said, stoutly. "And that goes for all of us Watchdogs! We have to be like federal agents. *They* never take bribes either!"

"So arrest me then!" sneered the wise guy. "And I bet that shirt isn't *real* silk! You're only wearing it to copy Felicity Snell, anyway!"

After that, he tried the same tactics with Ruth in the Adult Department, with the same result.

It was only up in the Natural History Museum that he thought he'd lucked out. Julie and Robyn were on duty in there. This time he approached his marks with his cheeks bulging with candy. It gladdened his heart to see the way their eyes bulged, too. Very promising!

And, sure, they accepted his M & M's, all right.

But they—alas for him—were two little tough cookies. For all they were so skinny and looked half-starved, they'd decided to teach him a lesson.

"It's what they call a sting operation," Julie whispered to Robyn behind the cover of a stuffed moose. "So let's do it. Cheat the cheat!"

So, with their mouths full of his M & M's, they sent him meandering around the hides and dens of other stuffed creatures with their directions of "warmer" or "colder" and "No, sorry. I meant, *cold*, freezing cold!" and "Correction! I meant hot, hot, hot! You're on fire!" until the poor guy's head began to spin and, once again, he gave up.

This was the wise guy's wisest move yet, because they could have gone on all day giving him misdirections and letting him walk right past (1) the working model of a beehive with its partly concealed yellow card, and (2) the sparrow's nest that contained a mother bird sitting on her five eggs and an amazing collection of scraps of wool, string, moss, and paper, including candy wrappers, rail tickets, half an envelope, an expired lottery ticket—and one red clue card.

But the worst cheating wasn't so easy to deal with—the kind attempted by the really sneaky ones who memorized the number and word on a card, then pushed it out of sight so no one else could have a chance of spotting it.

The Watchdogs had been warned about this, and made regular

checks to make sure that all cards were still visible, if only just. They had to be careful, though, in case some cheats kept watch on the Watchdogs and got to know the location of the clues that way!

Cheating or no cheating, however, all this made for the quiet, fairly smooth running of the contest for the first forty-five minutes or so.

In fact, it was Mary and the driver who made the most disturbance as the two of them went around selecting books for Mary's winter display—with Mary snapping at the poor man to wake up, or concentrate, and him grumbling at the growing pile he had to carry, and dropping them, and having to pick them up, saying why did she have to choose such heavy volumes.

"So take them out to the van before the piles get too big!" she snapped back. "And stop dropping them, butterfingers!"

He grumbled about that idea, too, saying it would take too much going in and out all morning—until he finally realized it would give him more chances to stop for a smoke.

Ruth actually saw him enjoying such an excuse one time.

Mary had selected one of the books in the Adult Department without noticing the narrow quarter-inch strip of red card poking out between the pages. The driver had taken the book away with his latest pile when Ruth realized what had happened.

She found him sitting in the parking lot, on the front bumper of his van, relaxing with a cigarette. Sweets was quite near, tugging at the back bumper of the old library van. On seeing Ruth, he set up a barrage of happy yelping barks, probably thinking she'd been sent by Spencer to bring him back with her.

But she had to return the red card quickly, so she said, "Sorry, Sweets! Gotta go back on duty!" before turning to the driver and telling him what she'd come for.

"It could have ruined the contest if the card had disappeared!" she explained.

"Gee! We wouldn't have *that* happen, would we?" said the man, as he blew out a gusty cloud of smoke and handed the card over. (It was Number Four and its word was *Arnold*.) "Don't forget to tell Mary it wouldn't have happened if she'd been more careful!"

"Yes, sir," said Ruth, who had no intention of passing on any such message, knowing how short-fused Mary could be.

She went back to the building with Sweets's reproachful barks following her.

The misplacing of *that* card had been a pure accident. But up in the Junior Room, Freddie and Holly Jenks were just then discussing what looked like a deliberate act of sabotage.

16

Sabotage by a Member of Staff?

They had discovered that the two red clue cards in the Video Department had been shoved out of sight, down behind the plastic-covered jackets of *Bambi* and *Moby Dick*.

Freddie had discovered it while Holly was still fighting off temptation in the Junior Room. He'd fished inside the jackets and put the cards back where Felicity had first placed them. Then he went back to warn Holly. The wise guy was just leaving. Holly listened to Freddie with growing indignation.

Five minutes later, she went into the Video Department to check for herself.

She came back before long.

"Are they still showing?" Freddie asked.

"They are *now*!" she said. "But when I went in, those cards had *already* been pushed right back out of sight!"

"So what did you do?"

"Put them back where they should have been. Naturally!"

"Did you see anyone do it?" asked Freddie.

"No. Everyone was up at the other end of the room. A bunch of kids were trying out some new video games that Mr. Vitalis had just released. Boys, mainly." Holly sniffed disdainfully. "They seem to have forgotten the contest already."

"Yeah, I bet," said Freddie, frowning. "He tried to get *me* interested, but I pointed to my Watchdog tag. Anyway, where was *he*?"

"Showing Mr. Rubinstein how the Internet works."

"Yeah," said Freddie, darkly. "He was doing that when *I* was in there. Was Ms. Twitchpurse still with him?"

"No, she was just leaving. . . . But young Benny Stockler was up at that end, looking for clue cards and getting Mr. Vitalis mad. In fact, he broke off talking to Mr. Rubinstein to tell Benny there were no clue cards up there—only at the other end among the *video* stands."

"Hm! D'you think *Benny* has been shoving the cards out of sight?"

"No!" Holly was beginning to flush with triumph. "*I* thought of that. So, before he went to search through the videos, I asked Benny if I could take a peek at his entry form. He didn't hesitate. He seems to have spotted more than half the cards already. But not Nine and Ten—the numbers in the Video Department. If he had, the spaces wouldn't have been left blank."

"Nice work, Holly!" But Freddie was still frowning. A grim but growing idea was beginning to form. . . .

He gave it another five minutes, then went back into the Video Department.

This time the cards had been left on view, just as Holly had left them. What's more, Freddie was just in time to see young Benny spot Number Nine, scribble the word down on his list (it was *letting*) and turn eagerly to scan the stacks for Number Ten. The kid, himself, didn't try to cheat, but replaced Number Nine exactly where he'd found it.

"I think I'm gonna win this contest!" he said.

So Benny is in the clear! thought Freddie, turning his attention to the person he was beginning more and more to suspect.

The kids at the other end were still playing with the new video games and Gary Vitalis was still talking to Mr. Rubinstein. Freddie quickly looked away. He found it difficult to stand the sight of Mr. Vitalis in his sharp suits, flashy silk ties, high white collars, and long white shirt cuffs, with gleaming white teeth to match. Freddie didn't care much for *them* either, always on show in a broad oily smirk whenever Ms. Twitchpurse or Mr. Hayes were around. Today, for Mr. Rubinstein, it seemed even oilier and showier.

No. Freddie didn't like Mr. Gary Vitalis, head of the Video Department. He never had. Not since the day he heard Vitalis tell one of his assistants, without even bothering to keep his voice down, "Don't let that Fisher kid near the handheld games. They're too easy to slip into a person's pockets, and we must never forget that his father's been in jail for thieving."

Despite all this, Freddie couldn't resist going along to take a look at some of the new games. He'd once been a keen player himself. His name was still on the main arcade's roll of honor downtown. "Fast Freddie," they used to call him.

Vitalis was still talking, as loudly as usual, to Mr. Rubinstein.

"Yes, sir," Freddie heard him say, "I could transform this entire corner into somewhere people could come to surf the Internet while their kids played good educational video games. Maybe we could serve coffee with it, too. Perhaps have Elaine from next door to look after that. . . . The Sip 'n' Surf Café, I'd call it. I'd section it off by hanging real fishing nets for curtains and borrow some surf boards for decoration . . . maybe from your Sports Department, sir. And maybe Mary Farrell could come along and make a really professional display of it. . . . It's all part of my vision for the future. The library as a Videotek for the New Millennium . . . where one picture would be worth a thousand words and a *motion* picture worth a million!"

Freddie couldn't take any more of this.

He went out of the room seething and thinking: *The creep! I wonder if Felicity knows he's plotting to poach Elaine from the Junior Department? I bet he hasn't shared his vision with her!*

Then he remembered Professor Ames's words and the thought struck him full force:

Hey! The guy's a member of staff, right? He seems to have some sort of grudge against Felicity, right? That's good enough for me! He's head of my Chameleon list of suspects now!

Then he shook his head. *Watch it, Freddie!* he told himself. *You're getting as bad as J.G.!*

"And *you* watch it, too!" he added—aloud this time—as his sister Ruth bumped into him.

"Sorry, Freddie!" Ruth blinked up at him. "I didn't see. . . . But listen. I think something very queer's been going on."

"Like what?" he said, looking anxiously toward the Junior Room door.

"I mean in the Adult Department. They . . . they've found some peanut brittle on one of the shelves. . . . Then I looked around myself. And found *three* more pieces! This is one of them. . . ."

With all unworthy thoughts of Vitalis clear gone from his head, Freddie stared at the sticky object in the palm of Ruth's hand.

He made a careful drawing of it later. This:

"Calm down and tell us all about it!" he said, steering her into the room to join Holly.

17

Elaine's Startling Discovery

Freddie chose the crime scene area for this. Elaine looked up from the counter but, seeing their Watchdog tags, just smiled and left them to their conference.

So they kept close together—Ruth, Freddie, Holly, and the "corpse"—while Ruth unfolded her account.

It had all happened in the last twenty minutes, she explained. The driver had returned, only to find that Mary had already chosen *another* pile of heavy books, including one on quilt making, which Mary said would look just fine in the window displaying winter evening hobbies.

They left still arguing, with Mary saying they'd better try the Reference Room next before he ran right out of steam. "The trouble with you is you smoke too much. I could smell it as soon as you walked in again."

"She was right, too," said Ruth. "I think I caught some of it in my hair, out in the parking lot!"

"Yes, you *did*," said Holly, with a sniff. "I was wondering where it was coming from. . . . But go on about the candy."

"Well, that old uncle of Ms. Fitch's found it. The one who's deaf and talks in a loud voice. The one who comes in here sometimes to borrow

Judy Blume books and cackles like a goose at the funny bits. . . ."

"Mr. Peabody, yes," said Freddie. "But *where*? Where did he find this candy?"

"Ready for this?" Ruth lowered her voice. "On the shelf *at the bottom of the stack where Oliver Twist used to be*!"

"Aha!" said Holly.

"Yes," said Ruth. "Now maybe you see why I was so interested when I heard him complaining." She raised her voice. " 'Some kid must have left it here!' he said. 'That's the trouble with letting them loose all over the library. Ms. Snell ought to know better! And so should Mr. Hayes for letting *her* have the run of the place for a stunt like this!' "

Elaine's smile broadened. Ruth had given a very good imitation of the crotchety old man. But the kids were dead serious, especially when Ruth went on to give her account, at Freddie's request, of who *else* had been around at the time: adults choosing books, kids looking for clue cards.

"But none of them seemed to notice anything wrong," said Ruth. "*I* did, though. I made a quick check and found three more pieces. All on bottom shelves in gaps between books. In different parts of the room: biography, great paintings, do-it-yourself. . . . *I* didn't hand them in at the counter, though. I thought I'd better leave them be and see if anyone came to check on them."

"Good thinking!" said Freddie. "That's just—"

"Excuse me!"

It was Elaine.

"I couldn't help overhearing," she said. "You're talking about a hunk of candy, right?"

Freddie nodded. "Four, to be precise."

"Well make that *five*," said Elaine. "There's one right there. Where the body's lying."

"Huh?"

An electric tingle seemed to run through all three kids.

"Just peeping out from under the dummy," said Elaine. "You can see it better from where *I* am."

They were already prowling around the "corpse," gingerly, like Scene-of-the-Crime officers themselves.

"I thought Mary or Felicity must have put it there," said Elaine. "As another clue."

"Gosh! Yeah!" Holly was pointing to a piece similar to Ruth's, with half its wrapper still intact, looking as if it had fallen from the dummy's back pocket.

They stared at each other, mystified, uneasy.

"What's going on?" whispered Holly.

"Beats *me*," said Freddie. "But I aim to find out!"

"*I* think," said Ruth, "that it has something to do with Spencer Curtis. I saw him filling his face with peanut brittle earlier, while Felicity was talking about the contest. And you know how he's always feeding bits of candy to Sweets, even though it isn't supposed to be good for dogs."

"Huh!" grunted Holly. "You try telling Spence that!"

"Anyway," said Ruth, "my idea is that Spencer might be trying to save some for Sweets before he eats it all himself. To stash it around where it's not within easy reach and won't be such a temptation."

"Hey, yes!" said Holly. "But talking of temptation, it *could* be Clyde Robbins."

"Who?" said Freddie.

"That older boy who tried to tempt me with candy to tell him where the clue cards were. It didn't work with *me*, but he could have decided to stash it as a reward for other Watchdogs who *might* be weak enough to help him."

"And then what?" said Freddie. "When he's stashed the . . . uh . . . rewards . . ."

"You know," Holly said. "Making a game of it. *Candy for Clue Cards*. 'You "warmer and colder" me to the cards, and I'll guide you to the candy.' Think of the trouble he'd cause with kids hunting for candy all over the place instead of cards!"

"Hm! A real act of sabotage!" Freddie murmured. "Crafty enough for The Chameleon himself!"

He was picturing a fascinating sight: Gary Vitalis on all fours, snooping around the bottom shelves planting his bait, with his latest flashy tie dangling loose like a lizard's long tongue flicking out to catch its prey.

Ruth broke into this vision. "Hey! I wonder if Mr. Peabody's The Chameleon! He isn't a member of the staff but he's a close relative of one. And he doesn't seem to like Felicity."

"I'm going to see if I can find out more about this peanut brittle from Spencer," Freddie said. "Right now!"

Telling Ruth to go back to the Adult Department and keep an eye on things there, and telling Holly to watch out for the return of Clyde Robbins "or anyone *else* acting suspiciously," he went straight upstairs, three at a time.

18

Orville Gets Restless

Up in the Reference Room, Tim and Spencer had been having a very uneasy time. They'd had Ms. Fitch to contend with as well as possible cheats.

If they moved too quickly, or spoke above a whisper, or kept going to the window as Spencer did, anxious to check on Sweets, she'd pull them up and tell them to be quiet, or to sit down, or come away from the window or from the Local Collection corner. Especially that last-named location!

If she told them once that the Local Collection was off-limits, she must have told them a dozen times. In the end, Tim suggested she put a couple of chairs in front of the Local Collection with a sign saying "Off-limits to all contestants. No clue cards beyond this point!"

That pleased her, anyway.

But she still kept fussing.

Ms. Fitch had taken it to heart that Ms. Twitchpurse's greatnephew had come to the Reference Room as a refuge from the hurly-burly of the contest, and she was very anxious to keep him happy.

The trouble was that you can't *keep* anyone happy when they're far from happy to begin with. And Orville, right from the start, had acted like one miserable, spoiled, restless brat. He'd spent about three minutes glancing at the Junior Room books that Felicity had carefully picked for him, and another ten complaining they were boring.

Then Ms. Fitch had run around trying to tempt him with books from the Reference Room shelves. But he soon grew tired of looking at pictorial collections of *Fighting Planes of Two World Wars*, of battleships, of butterflies, and of ladies' dresses through the ages. Even one on rare skin diseases that Spencer recommended, saying it had once caused Holly Jenks to faint and another kid to throw up when they snuck a look at it the time they'd been allowed in there on a school project last year. Ms. Fitch soon took it away from Orville.

But it didn't really matter.

Even that hadn't engaged the kid's interest.

No. What *he* wanted was to be left to go seeking clues like everyone else. After all, he'd already spotted the three flashes of red and one of gold that took care of the four cards allotted to the Reference Room. He felt sure it wouldn't take *him* long to get all the rest, including the "Go-right-to-the-top" one.

So Orville muttered and sighed and sat there sullenly until, finally, he thought he'd try a different angle and get to work on Ms. Fitch herself.

He'd noticed how concerned she'd been about the Local Collection.

"Ms. Fitch . . ."

"Yes, Orville—do please keep your voice down!"

"Sorry, ma'am. But what's that long funny-looking book in the glass case there?"

"Oh, that's very special."

"Does it have pictures?"

"Oh, no. That's the galley proofs of a very famous novel. Specially bound as a memento for the author's widow. A very rare and valuable item. We were lucky to acquire it. But thanks to the generosity of your great-aunt Gloria—"

"What are galley proofs? Like galley slaves?"

"Well . . . uh . . . not exactly . . ."

"May I see it?"

"Well, not out here. With all these people about." (Mary and the driver had just entered, closely followed by Freddie.) "But come with me, Orville," said Ms. Fitch.

Soon Orville was sitting by her side in front of the glass case and his voice was rising far above the level usually allowed.

"Gosh! I've never seen a book like *this* before, Ms. Fitch! You say Aunt Gloria gave it? . . . How much was it? A thousand dollars? . . . More! *How* much more?"

Someone tugged Tim's sleeve. Freddie.

"What's all *that* about?"

"Oh, nothing really," said Tim, grinning. "Just Orville getting into Ms. Fitch's good graces. You shoulda seen the way he softened her up."

Mary and the driver were already arguing, their voices getting louder. Even so, Ms. Fitch hadn't turned to ask them to be quiet.

"It just shows how well Orville's scheme is working!" said Tim.

"Yeah, well," said Freddie, looking around to where Spencer was. "I've come to ask Spence about—"

"Just a sec!" said Tim. Mary's hand was hovering in front of a bright yellow-covered book called *Brewer's Dictionary of Phrase and Fable*. A yellow card had been folded in half and was just sticking out from the spine, and Tim didn't want her to remove it accidentally. Then he relaxed as she picked another book instead. "This maroon and gold cover will just match the drapes in the soft furnishing display—here, take it," she said, putting it on top of the driver's growing pile.

"Huh!" he grunted. "And talking of soft furnishings, instead of this heavy book on quilts, why not borrow the old patchwork quilt in the Local History Museum? The—"

He broke off as Orville's voice rose.

"Twenty-five thousand dollars! Wow! Aunt Gloria *is* generous, Ms. Fitch!"

Mary took the opportunity to say, "If I need any ideas from *you*, Carl Green, I'll ask. Okay?"

"Well, sure," the driver replied humbly, "but I was thinking. If there was a *real* murdered stiff downstairs, they'd need to cover it when it's carried away on a stretcher, and the quilt would—"

"You're beginning to sound like that jerk kid brother of mine," said Mary. "But, hey, maybe you're right. Only they wouldn't use a prize exhibit, you schmuck! Some old dust sheet from the janitor's store would be all. Remind me when we take the dummy back. We might as well do it in style!"

The driver looked very pleased. Tim guessed it mustn't have been often that Mary accepted one of *his* ideas.

"Hey!" Spencer broke in. "What's with the peanut brittle, Freddie?"

"That's what I've come to ask *you* about! Uh . . . before it melts." The candy was beginning to get soft and sticky in Freddie's hand.

"You brung it for *me*?" asked Spencer. "Thanks, I'll—"

"Don't touch it!" snapped Freddie. "We don't know where it's been."

Spencer's eyes widened. "Huh?"

"Ruth found it in the Adult Lending Department. With some other pieces of candy just like it. She thought maybe *you*'d stashed it . . . You know? For Sweets, when you got around to releasing him. . . . What's wrong?"

Spencer had gone crimson to the tips of his ears. It looked like embarrassment at having to tell a lie, when he said, huskily, "I . . . I don't know what you're talking about, Freddie. Nothing to do with *me*. . . ."

But it was *guilt*, really, with poor Spencer feeling a world-class, rotten, dirty, all-time heel for not thinking of stashing some for his dog. Instead of scarfing it all himself!

"Anyway, I . . . we . . . me and Sweets . . . we don't use that brand. I . . . uh . . . we prefer the old fashioned kind that comes in bigger slabs . . . uh . . . like this. . . ."

He was digging into one of his pockets and finally pulled out a crumpled wrapper, as sticky as Freddie's, but empty, with only a few tiny slivers and chips of caramel adhering to it, along with a few balls of fluff from the bottom of his pocket.

Freddie made a careful drawing of it later, for the record. This one:

"You mean you never use Lone Star brand at all?" said Freddie.

By now, Tim had steered them both gently into the corridor, out of Ms. Fitch's earshot.

"Nargh!" said Spencer. "The fancy bite-size chunks are either too big or too small. Accordin' to whose mouth's doin' the biting. Armadillo brand, you can break it off just right. Dog bites or kid bites. Tastes better, anyway."

"Another theory," said Freddie, "is that it's been placed there as bait by the creep who wants to wreck the contest."

"Huh! Bait for who?" asked Tim.

"Well . . . maybe the Watchdogs."

"*Poisoned?*" gasped Spencer.

"I'm not saying *that*!" said Freddie. "That would be attempted murder, and even The Chameleon . . ."

Spencer's face had gone from beetroot red to chalk white. "But it wouldn't be murder if it was for an animal! What if it's bait for someone like Sweets? *He'd* go for it and—Hey! Have you heard him barking lately? I haven't!"

He hurried back into the Reference Room and straight to the window, nearly sending a chair flying.

"*Now* what?" came Ms. Fitch's exasperated cry.

Orville had turned around with her. "Yes, keep it down, you guys!"

Spencer ignored them both. "Come on," he said to Tim and Freddie. "Let's go into the museum! Better view of the parking lot from in there!"

They were already emerging into the corridor.

Then suddenly they froze.

They could hear barking *now*, all right!

Mixed in with Mr. Snerdoff's bellowing and a kid's yelling. All of it coming up from the lobby.

"It . . . it's *Sweets*!" gasped Spencer, peering over the banister. "Someone musta let him loose!"

19

Sweets on the Rampage

Spencer's gasp was followed by a surge of relief.

"He's *alive*!" he sang out.

The dog looked up. He'd just avoided the outstretched tattooed arms of the lobby's ferocious guardian. And now, who should Sweets see peering over the banister but his young master!

With a yelp of joy and ears flapping, he surged up the steps.

"Yah! You missed him again!" jeered a kid below, who sounded like Benny Stockler, as Ernest Snerdoff set off in ponderous pursuit.

By now, Sweets had leaped the last few feet into Spencer's arms. Sure, Spencer had left him tied to the back of a van, but as he licked the boy's burning cheeks, Sweets was more than ready to let bygones be bygones. And especially as his nose came closer to Spencer's mouth and he sniffed up a strong aroma of caramel.

Ah, yes! He knew that smell! The real thing this time.

The dog was now sniffing daintily around Spencer's fingers and—yes—it was strong there, too. So, next step . . .

But, as Sweets's wet nose began to probe into the right-hand pocket, those fingers tried to bar the way. . . .

The dog gave a puzzled little growl. *What was going on here?* His master usually liked this game of *Sniff out the Candy*!

By now Ernest Snerdoff was nearly upon them, gasping.

Sweets renewed his attempts to get into Spencer's pocket. Spencer renewed his efforts to prevent the dog from finding out how treacherous he'd been in eating all the peanut brittle himself.

"Now keep . . . tight hold . . . on him!" Snerdoff was saying, as Spencer tugged at Sweets's collar. "While I go get a rope . . . or something."

Spencer gave in. "Sorry, Sweets," he mumbled, as he pulled out the empty wrapper. "I guess you'd a found out sooner or later!"

For another second, as he sniffed eagerly at the crumpled paper, Sweets thought he'd won. But when he found nothing there but a crumb of candy and a piece of fluff that got up his nose and made him want to sneeze, his disappointment was overwhelming.

With a strange sound—part howl, part sneeze, part snarl of disgust—he turned to the other kid standing there: Freddie, with a smile of sympathy on his face and something interesting in his hand.

Freddie's pleasure had been at seeing the reunion between dog and boy. The something interesting had been the sticky piece of peanut brittle he'd almost forgotten about.

But Sweets hadn't. He knew very well he wasn't supposed to take treats from any hand but his master's.

Well, *phooey to that*!

The dog deftly snatched the candy from Freddie's hand, growled angrily, and tossed it in the air is if it were the corpse of a caramelized rat. Unfortunately, before he could catch it again, a tattooed hand shot out toward his collar.

"I told you to hold him tight!" Snerdoff grumbled at Spencer, but by then Sweets was on his way. Romping along the corridor, sidestepping J.G., who was hurrying toward the scene of the hubbub, diving between the legs of other kids, and yelping with recognition at the appearance of Julie and Robyn as they came running from the Natural History Museum.

The yelp changed into one of delight as he saw Robyn holding *another* hunk of candy just like the one he'd almost managed to snatch from Freddie. This one was also ready-peeled and all set to go. It must be a new kind of glorious game—*Peanut-brittle Galore*!

Well, he wasn't going to blow it this time!

He jumped at Robyn's hand and snatched the candy. This time he kept it firmly in his mouth. The girl screamed with surprise and fell back. Julie was making a lunge at the dog and her head bumped against Robyn's, whose nose got a glancing blow and immediately spurted blood. It wasn't a nasty blow and no bones were broken but Robyn bled easily. As soon as she felt the crimson flow running down her chin and spilling onto her white shirt, her screams redoubled. Simply with shock.

Robyn's head had been full of her find, which had been tossed into the nest of a stuffed grebe and her chicks, and she'd been running to find Freddie and show it to him. And now, in the blink of a tearful eye, here she was, her find whipped out of her hand and her shirt getting as red as Holly's.

Who was bending over her and saying, "Hush now, honey! Watchdogs don't cry!"

"They do when they've been mugged by vicious fugitive dogs!" said Julie, shouldering Holly away. "It's okay, Robyn. Just hold your head back, it'll soon stop bleeding!"

"A badly trained, loutish, juvenile offender dog!" said Ruth, who'd also come rushing to the scene. "I saw it happen. Was that a piece of candy he snatched off you? Where did you find it? It looked—"

"Who are you calling badly trained and a . . . a juvenile offender?" Spencer broke in. He'd heard Robyn's screams and seen the blood. Also the tail of his vanishing dog. He'd been anxious to make sure the girl wasn't badly hurt.

But he wasn't standing for *this*!

The dog's behavior was a touchy subject at the Curtis household. Sweets had been in trouble with the neighbors lately for barking and general over-boisterous behavior. He'd even done a stretch in the pound. He was in a three-strikes-and-you're-out situation.

The crowd had grown. The whole Watchdog Squad seemed to have deserted their posts. But then, so did the contestants seem to be deserting their quests. And now another crimson shirt had appeared. A very harassed-looking Felicity was crouching beside Robyn, who was on her feet but still dripping blood.

A flashbulb popped.

"Head well back, honey!" Felicity was saying soothingly. "It'll soon stop!"

"*I* told her that, Felicity!" said Julie.

"Good thinking, Julie," said Felicity.

J.G. now felt it was time he got into the act. "All right, folks!" He waved his pipe at the crowd. "Show's over! Move along and give the kid some air!"

"Hoo . . . !" Robyn moaned bravely as Felicity gave her a hug. She still had tears in her eyes, but she wasn't crying now. To be hugged by Felicity was worth losing a couple of gallons of blood any day.

"All right, don't make a meal of it!" murmured Julie, beginning to feel slightly jealous.

Someone else was murmuring too—Gloria Twitchpurse to Mr. Hayes:

"Great! This is all we wanted! The news photographers are still around and—*there*!"

Another flashbulb popped.

Robyn's white face stood out in the glare.

So did the red stains on her shirt.

Felicity hugged her closer to hide them from any further intrusive shots.

Then another white face stood out as a third flashbulb went off.

This time the subject was nowhere near Robyn herself. It was Orville, now edging away from the Reference Room at the back of the crowd.

Julie approached the cameraman. "Is our picture going to be in the paper, mister?"

The man pushed her aside. "Outa the way, kid! I gotta see where he's gone!"

Julie thought he meant the dog. Jealous as she'd been feeling, her Fisher blood was suddenly aroused. This made her exaggerate.

"Huh! You sound more interested in a dangerous dog than a little girl who's been bit by it and might be bleeding to death!"

The man looked at her sharply. "Dangerous, did you say? Was that a fact already known to these library people?"

"Well . . . ," grunted Julie, shrugging lamely. "I don't really know."

The man went on his way, past what was left of the crowd.

Felicity lost no more time after making sure that Robyn was feeling better. Calling the Watchdogs to her side, she found out the main details about Sweets's reappearance and the stashed pieces of candy. Then she turned to J.G., Ruth, and Tim, and asked them to go down to the parking lot to see what happened to the dog's leash. Also to check with Mary and the driver if *they'd* seen anything down there.

"Consider it done, Felicity," said J.G.

"What about *me*?" said Spencer.

"You come with me and help me catch Sweets," said Felicity. "We can't afford any more disturbance! And you others," she said, addressing the remaining Watchdogs, "go to your posts and keep a look-out for any strange behavior!"

The dark cloud had returned to her face.

"She's worrying about The Chameleon again!" guessed Freddie. "And no wonder! With the place in an uproar, the Watchdogs squabbling, and even the Chief Librarian getting it in the neck from Ms. Twitchpurse, that old Chameleon must have been really enjoying this last half hour! Laughing himself sick, I bet!"

He hurried off downstairs, hoping to get a glimpse of Gary Vitalis and see how *he'd* been taking all this. . . .

Down in the parking lot, there were plenty of people about by now, but no one seemed to be loitering near the old van.

"But *someone* must have been," said J.G. grimly, studying the leash still drooping forlornly from the back bumper. It had been tied there with a huge knot, all loops and twists and secondary knots. He poked at it with the stem of his pipe.

"Enough for a *tiger*!" he grumbled.

"So what?" said Ruth. "Whoever let Sweets loose didn't bother about the knots. He just unclipped the dog's collar. Like this." She reached out and pressed the spring clip at the end of the leash. "Simple!"

"And much safer!" mused J.G.

"Huh?" The others looked at him.

J.G. was already studying the tarmac nearby. "Sure. Ever tried going this near the teeth of a tied-up dog that's getting restless and annoyed?"

"But Sweets wouldn't *bite* anyone!" said Ruth.

"No, but everyone doesn't know that," said J.G. "Even *I* wouldn't go near his collar when he was as upset as that. Not without . . ."

He reached out and picked up something from the ground.

"Not without *what*?" said Tim.

"Some insurance," said J.G., smoothing out the scrap of paper he'd just picked up.

"The same kind as the candy stashed in the library!" said Ruth. "Except this hasn't been torn in half."

"No," said J.G. "He'd have started with the full bite-size until the dog calmed down."

"He certainly took his time making sure," said Ruth. "Look. Two, three, four—five more of the same wrappers! Like someone had been *feeding* the dog with the stuff."

"Come on!" said J.G.. "Let's see if Mary and Carl saw anything. I would have. As soon as the barking stopped."

"Sure you would . . . ," muttered Ruth, winking at Tim and waving an imaginary pipe as they followed their leader.

The driver was helping Mary check the books they'd collected. "Me? Looking out for dogs?" he said. "No time—all the work *we've* had to do!"

"Huh!" grunted Mary, looking up from her list. "All the work *I've* had to do, he means! All *he's* had to do is carry these books out!"

"I didn't see no dog anyway!" muttered the driver.

Ruth frowned. "*I* did! And he was only a few feet away when I came out to see you. Barking his head off!"

The driver frowned. "Oh, *that* dog! I thought you was looking for a mutt running around loose. *That* one was tied up."

"Yeah!" said J.G. *"Was!"*

"And was it *you* . . . ?" Ruth was going to say, "And was it you who's been giving it candy?"

But just then Elaine appeared, with Spencer and Sweets himself—now on a makeshift leash: Spencer's belt.

"We've come to pick up his usual leash, before Spencer here loses his trousers," Elaine said, grinning. "Felicity's asked me to run him and Sweets home in my car."

"I cornered him," said Spencer. "But it was Felicity who caught him and calmed him."

Sweets certainly looked peaceful now as he turned his head from one to another, listening.

"Calmed him with more of this?" said J.G., holding up one of the wrappers.

Sweets blinked innocently as if it meant nothing to *him*.

"No," said Spencer. "Felicity doesn't hold with"—he glanced cautiously at his dog—"c-a-n-d"—he mouthed the letters, leaving out the *y* in his anxiety—"for dogs. It was something to do with the way she held him and talked to him."

"Her training as a veterinarian's assistant," Elaine explained. "When she was working undercover. Anyway, let's get him away from any more mischief."

"Where is Felicity now?" asked Ruth, giving Sweets's ears a forgiving fondle.

"Busy," said Elaine. "Something urgent has cropped up."

"What?" asked J.G.

"I don't know. Something to do with the contest. Also the Natural History Museum."

"The Natural . . . ?" began J.G., looking perplexed.

"Yes," said Elaine. "A lizard's escaped from the terrarium. She said something about a chameleon. Uh . . . that *is* a lizard, isn't it?"

"Come on!" said J.G. to the other two, leaping out of the van so suddenly it set Sweets to barking again.

20

The Laughing Chameleon

When J.G., Ruth, and Tim got back, they found Felicity and the others at the crime scene. Benny Stockler was also present.

They all looked shaken and very grave—except Robyn, who was looking positively radiant and blissful.

This was partly because she'd been allowed to perch on the counter, presumably in honor of her invalid status, recovering from the alarming nosebleed. Also because of the voluminous bright yellow shirt she was wearing, which, on her, looked more like a nightgown.

It gave Ruth quite a shock to see her like that, up there, as if Julie had been right and their little sister had indeed bled to death and was now an angel on Cloud Nine.

"Hi, Ruthie!" the angel sang out as the breathless newcomers arrived. "Look at *me*! Felicity's lent me one of *her* shirts while mine's getting the blood soaked out of it!"

Even Ruth felt a slight pang of envy. As for Holly and Julie, for once, the skinny, agile Julie and the plump, awkward Holly had something in common. Both were eating their hearts out!

As for Benny, he looked as if he wouldn't have been interested if Robyn had started sprouting wings. His attention was focused on the entry form that Felicity was holding. He looked scared, petrified, and deeply guilty.

Very few contestants came in to disturb this council of war. Those who did show their faces soon turned away when they saw Felicity's expression as she lifted a hand in a "Sorry, kids, not now!" gesture.

J.G. thought of the field day the cheats must be having in other rooms with no Watchdogs around.

Felicity must have read his thoughts. "That's okay, John," she said. "There are much bigger things to worry about *now*!"

"Like what, Felicity?" he asked. "What *has* happened?"

"This!" said Felicity grimly, shaking the entry form.

Poor Benny flinched.

"But Elaine said it was something about The Chameleon!" said J.G. "Running about on the loose!"

"She was right!" said Felicity.

"Have you *seen* The Chameleon, then?" Tim asked, wide-eyed.

"Is it Clyde Robbins?" asked Holly.

"Mr. Peabody?" Ruth put in.

"Mr. Vitalis?" asked Freddie, hopefully.

"Or the photographer with the flashbulbs?" asked Julie, with a look of triumph at Robyn and Ruth, seeing her chance to shine at last.

"Oh, *him*!" said Felicity, smiling wryly. "The big, dark-haired guy with a bushy black mustache? I don't think so, Julie. I've had my eye on *him* all morning."

"Really, Felicity?" said J.G. His pipe was out for this.

"Yes," said Felicity. "He's a private investigator. Not a very honest one, either. Snooping on Orville and his mother. Probably hired by Orville's dad. But no. *He* isn't The Chameleon."

This had them all baffled, especially J.G.

"Well, is it *him* then?" he said, jabbing the pipe stem at Benny. "That's *his* entry form, isn't it?" J.G. had recognized the messy, sprawling writing.

"Leave me be, you big bully!" wailed Benny, aiming a kick at his tormentor and missing. "I didn't do *nothing*!"

Hot tears were beginning to spill.

"Take it easy, Benny," murmured Felicity. "Nobody's accusing you of anything!"

"*Yet!*" growled J.G., still fixing Benny with his merciless gray eye.

"No," said Felicity, addressing them all. "I haven't actually seen The Chameleon. But we have heard from that person. Or as good as."

"Heard *what*?" asked J.G., glancing uneasily at the telephone.

"He or she's been in direct communication with us," said Felicity. "Within the last hour. No, not on the phone, John. On Benny's entry form, in fact."

She pointed to the list of words, tapping her finger next to number four:

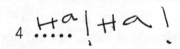

"Looks like Benny's writing to *me*!" said J.G.

Benny was now crying openly.

"It is," said Felicity. "But Benny isn't to blame. He was only doing his contest things. (Hush, Benny!) Properly."

"But . . . but *that* isn't properly, Felicity," said Ruth. "The word for Number Four is a name—*Arnold*."

"Is it?" said Felicity. She'd produced the red card and was holding it out. Ruth goggled at it.

#4   "Ha! ha!"

"But I saw this very card half an hour ago!" protested Ruth. "This wasn't stuck on it then!" She began to pick at the scrap of laughter, and peeled some of it away to reveal the original *Arno—*.

"Leave it!" snapped J.G. "There may be fingerprints!"

"Oh, I doubt *that*!" said Felicity. "It seems too smudged."

"Whose fingerprints?" asked Ruth.

"He means The Chameleon's," said Felicity. "If they could be brought out clearly."

"The Cham—?" began Ruth.

"How did *you* come to see it, Ruth?" asked Felicity, taking the card from her. "Was it when you were in the Adult Lending Department?"

"No. Out in the parking lot," said Ruth.

"And was it still untampered with?" asked Felicity, keenly.

"Yes," said Ruth. "Number Four—*Arnold*."

"So this must have been stuck on in the last half hour or so!" said J.G.

"Which proves what I've been saying," said Felicity. "The Chameleon is actually on the premises right now. Which also makes that person definitely the prime suspect for the candy stashes."

"Gosh, yeah!" gasped Tim. "That's his M.O., isn't it? Making a disturbance using loose animals. First, the ferret! Then, the white rats! And now, Sweets!" He swung to Felicity. "Has there been anything valuable . . ."

"Stolen?" said Felicity. "No. Not so far, anyway. I've checked with Mr. Hayes. He'd been keeping close watch on his office while there was all the excitement over Sweets. Double-locking it when he had to leave it even for a minute. . . . Yes, Benny. Go ahead."

When Felicity allowed Benny to correct his entry form, he looked up. "Who is Arnold, anyway?" he asked.

"*He* is," said Felicity, pointing to the "corpse." "Or was. Arnold Cripps." She frowned. "I thought Elaine had made out a name tag for Mary to pin on his shirt."

"She did," said J.G. "But Mary rejected it. She said an assistant janitor wouldn't be wearing it when he was off duty late at night. Which he was supposed to be when he was murdered."

Felicity shrugged. "Makes sense, I suppose. But what did she do with the tag?"

J.G. looked around. "I guess she put it back on the counter when she was clearing up. Hey, move over," he said to Robyn.

"*I* haven't sat on it," said the girl.

"Never mind," said Felicity. "Maybe Elaine's put it in a drawer." She was rummaging in one now. Shaking her head, she continued, "That's the least of our worries. What we have to do, right now— the whole squad—is check every clue card and make sure no more have been tampered with." She closed the drawer.

She had taken out a bunch of blank clue cards, red and yellow, and a small folding pocket magnifier, like the ones they used on field trips for studying flowers or bugs.

A thrill ran through the Watchdogs.

It was as if the sheriff in an old Western had just strapped on his gunbelt after spending his time trying to organize a peaceable rodeo, which some mysterious and elusive enemy had been bent on destroying.

Uncannily, the clock on a nearby church tower began to strike.

It was only eleven but to some of Felicity's posse of Watchdogs, it might as well have been twelve.

High noon, indeed!

The Chameleon had certainly been busy in the last couple of hours. He had struck in practically every one of the main rooms.

The Junior Room itself had been hard hit.

The Number One clue card—the red one in the spine of the almanac—had been left untouched, but Number Sixteen, the yellow card among the black-eyed Susans, had suffered. Its word, *ending*, had been obliterated by a peal of ha! ha! ha!'s—as if The Chameleon had said, "And that's just for openers!"

The same fate had befallen two of the red cards.

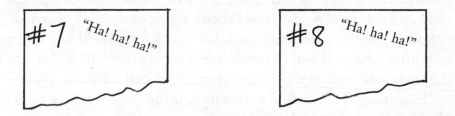

In the Adult Lending Department, another red card had suffered besides Number Four *Arnold*. On number Five, the laughter had been stuck on upside down, as if The Chameleon had been rolling over on his back in paroxysms of laughter.

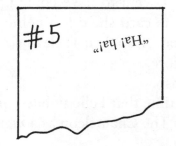

Much to Freddie's disappointment, the Video Department had so far escaped; cards Number Nine and Number Ten had not been tampered with. But the two red cards in the Newspaper and Magazine Room had been given the treatment, while up in the Reference Room both the yellow one in *Brewer's Dictionary of Phrase and Fable* and a red one revealed fits of Chameleon mirth.

("But where's Orville?" wondered Tim, glancing around as the others stared at these latest ha! ha!'s)

Next door, the Natural History Museum had completely escaped. The red card was still decorating the sparrow's nest and the yellow was still camouflaged against the model beehive.

Even so, by the time they finally reached the Third Floor, they seemed to have been pursued everywhere by ghostly laughter—from furtive titters, oily chuckles, and evil snickers to outright guffaws and maniacal peals—and Felicity was looking very worried.

So far, for every laughing card that was found, she'd left a clean one, after writing down its number and the correct word. She'd put the mutilated card in a clean envelope, very carefully.

"Evidence," Felicity had murmured, using the magnifier to give Number Seven's "Ha! ha! ha!" a second thoughtful scrutiny. "I think I know where this laughter is coming from. But I'll give it closer attention later."

After that, she said no more, but pressed on with the search, subjecting each new find to the same process.

"At least he doesn't seem to have come up this far," she said as she plucked out the card she'd left behind the nameplate on Mr. Hayes's office door. It looked as clean as when she'd placed it there the evening before.

Freddie stifled a gasp.

This was the first time that Felicity had come right out and so positively referred to The Chameleon as a *man*!

J.G. was staring at her.

Ruth had taken off her glasses and had frozen in the act of polishing them.

Tim was frowning.

Holly looked perplexed.

But even as they were reacting in their different ways, the phone inside the office burst out with its own brand of shrill laughter, making them jump, and they heard Mr. Hayes kill it with the murmur "Yes? Chief Librarian here. . . ." followed immediately by his roar of "WHAT? On the *ROOF*? *OUR* roof? A . . . a . . . BOY?"

It seemed that Felicity had spoken too soon!

21

Panic on the Roof

When Mr. Hayes answered the phone, he had no idea of the bombshell about to burst.

"Yes? Chief Librarian here. . . ."

He'd had a grueling morning, but his voice was calm enough. A bit curt, maybe. But civil and friendly.

Then the bombshell.

"There's a kid on your roof."

A man's voice. Also fairly calm. But what was he *saying*? The horror began to dawn. . . .

"WHAT? On the *ROOF*?" Mr. Hayes looked up—almost as if there'd been a nuclear bomb and, in its terrible flash, he could see through the ceiling. "*OUR* roof? A . . . a . . . *BOY*?"

The caller had said "kid," but somehow, Mr. Hayes had guessed it was a boy. Benny Stockler had been the one to come straight to mind.

The caller now sounded urgent. "You better do something quick! I already dialed nine-one-one. But if he falls off . . ."

Mr. Hayes did something quick. He rushed from the room, calling out, "Ms. Snell! Ms. . . ."

"Yes, Mr. Hayes?"

He pulled up with a jerk. He hadn't expected her to be so close. A break at last!

"Oh good! There's been a phone call. A child's gotten himself onto the roof. Benny Stockler, I think . . ."

"No, sir," said Felicity. "Benny's right here."

Young Benny's face was staring up at him, just as it had done when seeking the golden yellow card behind his handkerchief— Good gracious!—was it only two hours ago?

"Don't worry, sir," Felicity was saying. "I'll take a look up there myself. You others, see if you can find Mr. Snerdoff anywhere around. . . ."

"Thanks! I'll do that myself!" Mr. Hayes said, turning to the main stairs as Felicity headed off toward the back stairs leading to the roof.

He found Ernest Snerdoff in the lobby, listening with open mouth to the gabblings of a couple of kids who'd just rushed in.

"With me, Snerdoff!" said his boss, grabbing him by the sleeve and making for the door without even stopping, "Right now!"

In another two seconds, they were both out on the street gaping up at the building with a dozen or so rubberneckers. The banner was still fluttering against the blue sky and the questionmark cards were still gently swaying against the ivy.

But there was now a new element in the scene.

A boy—older and bigger than Benny—clinging to a ladder, half way to the top of the spire to which the left-hand side of the banner had been fastened.

And now Mr. Hayes thought he could hear cries.

"Help meee! Help meee!"

It had sounded like a seagull's call, at first. But it was the boy, all right. He had started to wave. Mr. Hayes shut his eyes, the kid looked so unstable.

"It . . . it's that new pilgrim, I think," said Ernest Snerdoff. "How'd *he* get up there?"

"How would *I* know?" snapped Mr. Hayes, more rattled than ever.

The thought that this could be the Chairperson's delicate great-nephew, in real peril of plummeting to his death, made the Chief Librarian break into a cold sweat.

"Don't just stand there, man!" he yelped.

Just then, a bright red shirt appeared on the battlements.

"That's Ms. Snell, sir!"

"I can see that! Get up there now in case she needs a hand!"

There was now the sound of fire engines, their warning blares still some distance away but getting nearer.

Mr. Hayes felt a warm wave of relief. But the sound of ambulance sirens soon chilled it.

Ernest Snerdoff had already gone back into the library, but a voice in the crowd did nothing to steady Mr. Hayes's nerves.

"She could get *herself* killed! Why doesn't she wait for the Fire Department?"

Felicity was now climbing up the ladder to get alongside the boy. The ladder seemed to be lurching. Maybe it wouldn't be strong enough to bear them both. Or was the fool kid panicking? His mother had said he was of a nervous disposition, hadn't she?

Mr. Hayes wondered what all this was doing to his *own* nerves! He gave another yelp when a pessimistic rubbernecker said, "They might be too late anyway!"

The boy was definitely struggling. Felicity was pinning him to the ladder, clamping his arms as best she could.

"What's she doing now?" said a woman's voice. "I just daren't look!"

"Me, either!" thought the Chief Librarian.

"She's clipped him one, I think!" replied a man.

Horrified, Mr. Hayes forced himself to look.

Orville did seem to have gone limp. Felicity seemed to have braced herself to take the extra weight.

"Best thing she could do," the wiseacre was saying. "Like when someone's drowning and thrashing around."

"What? At fifty feet above the ground?" someone else said.

Then the first flashes went off, somewhere on the roof.

A woman cried, "Oh, it's lightning! That's *all* they need!"

Mr. Hayes groaned. He knew it couldn't be a thunderstorm on a day like this. It was worse! As a third flash lit up the battlements, he realized what it was.

Flashbulbs!

Publicity!

His job! . . .

The crowd had now swollen. Most of the kids from the contest seemed to be there. Gary Vitalis was still jabbering away at Mr. Rubinstein without even glancing roofward. Did that jerk never think of *anything* except his vision for the all-electronic library of the future?

Elaine and Spencer weren't so callous. They'd just returned, and were staring up in horror.

And now Emily Fitch came rushing up.

"Oh, Mr. Hayes, Mr. Hayes! Ms. Twitchpurse's niece's boy . . ."

"I know, I know!" he said grimly. "Felicity's already taking care of it."

"If she can hold him *still*!" said Emily Fitch.

"The Fire Department's here now, anyway," said Mr. Hayes. "And hey . . . look! The cherry picker!"

As the apparatus began to climb higher and higher and nearer and nearer, a great combined sigh of relief, and not a few prayers, went up with it. . . .

Mrs. Eleanor Grisson had been feeling very happy when she left the Cuts 'n' Curls Salon a little earlier. Mrs. Kowalski had done a beautiful job on her hair.

A touch gabby, perhaps, mused Eleanor. But that was only after she'd mentioned the woman's son, Tim, and said she'd left Orville in his care. Every mother had the right to sing the praises of her only son. Eleanor herself was no exception, and soon they were both exchanging holiday snaps under the dryer: Mrs. Kowalski, pictures of the smiling fair-haired Tim, and she herself of the pasty, rather surly Orville, who hated having his photograph taken.

And when she mentioned that the Junior Librarian had taken the newcomer under her wing, the hairstylist had lit up again.

"Oh, Felicity Snell! My! *She's* something else!" she'd begun, and then went on with a litany of praise. All about Felicity's once being a private investigator and how the kids thought the world of her. And so on and on, blah! blah! blah!

But it didn't seem to interfere any with the woman's hairstyling skills, and Eleanor Grisson had left behind a handsome tip.

The glow of contentment didn't last long, however.

It began to fade when the blare of fire trucks broke in on her and she'd had to pull over to make way for the leading truck.

It was obviously heading in the same direction as she was.

She only hoped it wasn't the library!

But there was no smoke ahead. The sky was as clear and blue as when she'd left earlier.

"Silly *me*!" she thought.

And now that she was on West Main with still no sign of smoke, she almost laughed aloud.

Almost . . .

Because, as she rounded the bend, she saw the cherry picker's platform on its upward journey and the growing crowd on the sidewalk and—oh! Good heavens!—someone seemed to be up there on the roof, stranded!

Now she hoped fervently, as she slowed to a crawl, that Orville wasn't in that crowd. She would have to give him a good talking-to if he was! He knew very well that too much excitement was bad for his nerves, and—

A bang on the roof of the car made her pull up sharply.

A fire marshal was standing there with someone she suddenly recognized.

"Oh, hello, Aunt Gloria!" she said. "Has a kitten gotten itself stranded . . . ?"

"Don't get up from your seat, ma'am," the man warned.

Eleanor Grisson was now watching her aunt's face. It was chalk-white and strained.

Then, with a sudden rush, she began. "Eleanor, don't worry, everything's being taken care of but . . ."

That *but* did it. It made Eleanor look harder at the two figures on the ladder. The one in the red shirt seemed very familiar all at once, and now the other, being pinned by her . . .

Mrs. Grisson gave a scream of total recognition.

"Orville!"

Just before she went out like a light.

22

Outrage in the Reference Room

At twelve thirty, shortly after Orville and his mother had been rushed to the hospital, Felicity sat with Mr. Hayes in his office.

"*Did* you hit him?" asked Mr. Hayes.

"Of course not!" She felt in need of a shower and a change of shirt herself, and she was very hungry.

"I thought maybe he was panicking and you had to . . ."

"No," she said. "I reached out to his neck at one point. To check his pulse and give him some firm support there—oh, come on, Mr. Hayes! There's no time for details right now. How about *you*? Was anything stolen while everyone was outside?"

"Uh . . . no. Not as far as I've been able to . . ."

"Well, don't relax too soon. That guy isn't finished yet, believe me!"

"Did you get anything out of Orville? About how he came to be up there?"

"Only fragments," said Felicity. "But I did get him to talk a little, if only to take his mind off the drop."

"I can imagine!" Mr. Hayes shivered. "But go on. *What* fragments?"

"When the hospital releases him, we'll probably get a fuller statement," said Felicity. "In the meantime, I'm working on the scraps."

"And?"

"Well, the most I got out of him was that he'd been shown the way up by a . . . uh . . . janitor."

Mr. Hayes nearly jumped out of his chair.

"*Snerdoff?*"

Felicity shook her head. "I doubt that very much, sir. Ernest was down in the lobby when you found him, wasn't he?"

"Yes. But you said Orville had said a *janitor*. Who else *could* it have been? Unless the kid was hallucinating?"

"No," said Felicity. "He seemed very positive. Except . . ."

She wasn't really prepared to go further. Mr. Hayes was obviously still in shock himself.

But when she came to think of it, she had to admit that it did seem rather weird when Orville had said, "Yes. A janitor. It was on his name tag, *Arnold* Something. *Assistant Janitor.*"

For a few seconds up there, Felicity had felt her own head begin to spin. She'd had a vision of the dummy coming to life—like a zombie or Frankenstein's monster—and plodding up to the Third Floor to lure Orville to his death!

That was one of the things she was working on. Going over it again and again.

She went over it one more time now. . . .

It seemed that this zombie—this guy, this imposter—had seen Orville snooping around outside the janitor's storeroom, looking for the Number Twenty card. And the guy had told him "Right to the top" meant higher than that. "But come with me and I'll show you," he'd told Orville.

Felicity shared *that* much with Mr. Hayes.

He looked up sharply. "The roof?"

"Yes, sir."

"And the young sucker *followed* him?"

"Why not? Orville was a newcomer and *he* didn't know there

was no such person working here. And he *was* very eager to show all those kids who'd been jeering 'Awful Orville' at him how bright and tough he really was. Personally, I couldn't help admiring him for it!"

"Please, Felicity, don't let his mother hear you say that. But go on . . ."

"Well, when the man showed him the ladder and said the most important clue card was up there, tied to the spire, Orville couldn't wait and asked the guy to hold the ladder steady for him. When the guy agreed, Orville started up confidently enough."

Mr. Hayes had buried his head in his hands.

"Are you all right, sir?"

"Yes. Go on . . ."

"But when Orville glanced down and saw the man had deserted him, he panicked immediately and started yelling for help."

"He could have been killed right then!" groaned Mr. Hayes.

Felicity nodded grimly. "I'm afraid The Chameleon just doesn't care about reckless endangerment."

"The . . . The . . . Chameleon . . . ?"

But before Felicity could reply, there was an almighty crash at the door, and Emily Fitch burst in.

"Mr. Hayes! Come quickly! The Henry Charles manuscript! The leather-bound galley proofs that cost the library a fortune only two weeks ago! They . . . they've been stolen!"

"We're on our way!" said Felicity.

When they got to the Reference Room, they found Tim and Spencer looking shaken but standing on guard at the door.

Felicity and Mr. Hayes made straight for the Local Collection, where the door of the glass cabinet had been left wide open.

"Don't touch a thing!" said Felicity.

There wasn't much *to* touch anyway. All that was left was the space where the strange long manuscript had been displayed. Also the card with its description.

Or what was left of that, too.

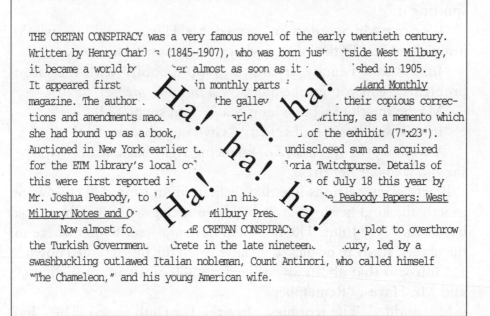

THE CRETAN CONSPIRACY was a very famous novel of the early twentieth century. Written by Henry Charl s (1845-1907), who was born jus+ 'tside West Milbury, it became a world b   'er almost as soon as it '   'shed in 1905. It appeared first   in monthly parts '   ⸰land Monthly magazine. The author   the galle   . their copious correc-tions and amendments mad   erl   writing, as a memento which she had bound up as a book,   of the exhibit (7"x23"). Auctioned in New York earlier t   undisclosed sum and acquired for the ETM library's local c⸰   'oria Twitchpurse. Details of this were first reported i   of July 18 this year by Mr. Joshua Peabody, to   in his   e Peabody Papers: West Milbury Notes and O   Milbury Pres

    Now almost fo   ⸏E CRETAN CONSPIRAC   plot to overthrow the Turkish Government   Crete in the late nineteen   cury, led by a swashbuckling outlawed Italian nobleman, Count Antinori, who called himself "The Chameleon," and his young American wife.

"The Chameleon!" gasped Felicity.

It wasn't just the large, grotesque "Ha! ha! ha!'s" that had been stuck there like a crossbones without a skull. Felicity's eye was arrested by that name in the last line of type on the card.

It was as if the mocking thief had used it as a signature!

"The guy must be totally raving mad!" said Mr. Hayes.

"He seems to think it's amusing, anyway," said Felicity.

"Why wouldn't he?" said Emily Fitch, with anger, despair, and panic in her voice. "If he's getting away with something worth twenty-five thousand dollars?"

She didn't add, "And nobody here to *stop* him!"

But it was there in her voice along with the rest.

"Who says he's gotten away with it, Ms. Fitch?" said Felicity. "He can't have carried off a bulky object like that without anyone spotting it."

"It's a pity Mr. Snerdoff isn't armed, Mr. Hayes," said J.G., who'd just walked in. "With orders to shoot if necessary. I know I . . ."

"John," said Felicity, trying to grapple coolly with the latest problems, "will you just be quiet for a minute, *please*!"

"Maybe the thief wore a long coat?" Tim suggested.

"In this weather?" said Felicity. "Give me a break, Tim!"

"A woman, then," said J.G., bouncing right back again. "Maybe she hid it under her dress."

Practical suggestions like that, Felicity didn't mind. Those were exactly the kind her own brain had been racing with. But she shook her head. "No, John. The thief will have stashed it somewhere in the library, ready to be picked up later when the fuss has died down."

"You said that about an earlier Chameleon incident, Felicity," said Mr. Hayes. "Remember?"

She nodded. The trophies, after the Pet Club fiasco. The Chameleon was probably thinking of pulling something like that again—spiriting the Charles manuscript out disguised as something else. But what? He couldn't shove it in a box with air holes and pretend it was hamsters this time!

The Chameleon would think of *something*. That was for sure. Something very clever. Something people wouldn't think about twice—until it was too late and the manuscript was long gone.

She sighed. The best thing would be to find it while it was still hidden on the premises.

"It might be stashed in this very room!" said J.G., stoutly backing Felicity up. He even pulled out his pipe to wag it at Mr. Hayes and

Ms. Fitch. "What better place to hide a book than among thousands of other books?"

"Yes, but a book *that* size?" said Ms. Fitch, as some of the others began to surge toward the shelves, with J.G. to the fore as usual.

Then she turned. "Excuse me, Ms. Snell. I know you said not to touch anything, but I just can't bear to see this horrible laughter. I have a duplicate card. Do you mind if I put it in the place of "— she gave a shudder—"*this?*"

Felicity couldn't see what good that would do. But it wouldn't harm to have a reasonable undamaged description of the stolen article. Especially if it helped calm the Reference Librarian down.

"Sure, why not, Ms. Fitch?"

She put the mutilated card in an envelope to join the laughter-ruined clue cards collected earlier. Then, after Ms. Fitch had put the duplicate card in its rightful place in the cabinet, she studied the original wording:

THE CRETAN CONSPIRACY was a very famous novel of the early twentieth century. Written by Henry Charles (1845-1907), who was born just outside West Milbury, it became a world best-setter almost as soon as it was published in 1905. It appeared first as a serial in monthly parts in the New England Monthly magazine. The author's widow kept the galley proofs, with their copious corrections and amendments made in Henry Charles's own handwriting, as a memento which she had bound up as a book, hence the unusual size of the exhibit (7"x23"). Auctioned in New York earlier this year for an undisclosed sum and acquired for the ETM library's local collection by Ms. Gloria Twitchpurse. Details of this were first reported in the West Milbury Gazette of July 18 this year by Mr. Joshua Peabody, to be reprinted in his pamphlet, The Peabody Papers: West Milbury Notes and Queries / West Milbury Press.

   Now almost forgotten, THE CRETAN CONSPIRACY was about a plot to overthrow the Turkish Government in Crete in the late nineteenth century, led by a swashbuckling outlawed Italian nobleman, Count Antinori, who called himself "The Chameleon," and his young American wife.

"I wonder . . ." she murmured.

"*What*, Felicity?" asked J.G.

"Oh, nothing, really, but . . ."

Emily Fitch saved Felicity from further questioning by saying, "The movie rights to the novel have just been bought. By Twentieth Century Fox, I believe."

"Yes," said Felicity. "I read about that at the hairdresser's. It's going to be a major production. It should cause a big revival in the sales of the novel."

"Not to mention doubling or trebling the auction value of the stolen manuscript!" said Mr. Hayes glumly.

Felicity now came to the question she'd been wondering about. "Did your uncle say anything about this in his piece for the *Gazette*, Ms. Fitch?"

"Yes, I'm almost sure he did," was the reply.

Great! thought Felicity. *Now we're getting somewhere!*

23

Elaine's Vital Information

At two-thirty that afternoon, Felicity Snell was still wondering how The Chameleon might be planning to get the Charles manuscript out of the building.

There were certainly plenty of eyes watching out for the long bulky book. The contest had been put off to a later date and all the Watchdogs were free to concentrate on this new search.

They'd even been joined by reinforcements. Kids who'd come along that morning to search for make-believe clues were now deputized to look for the real thing. Even some of the cheats had offered their services.

That had been J.G.'s idea.

Felicity had to hand it to him for *that*!

The kids who'd looked bitterly disappointed when they heard of the postponement over the public address system (some even cried), had actually cheered aloud when they heard J.G.'s voice follow Mr. Hayes's and ask for volunteers.

"Now hear this! Leader of the Watchdog Squad speaking. Please report to the Junior Room immediately if you're interested in looking for a really *vital* clue to a *real* crime perpetrated by a mysterious person who's been trying to wreck our library! Are we going to let him?"

Cries of "No!" and "No way!" had come from every part of the building, like heavenly music to Felicity's ears.

Mr. Hayes had looked alarmed.

But he needn't have worried.

Felicity glanced at her watch. The Watchdogs and their delighted deputies may not have found the missing manuscript yet, but they'd certainly gone about their search in an orderly way—one that left no room for any kind of boisterous clowning.

In fact, it made for a kind of uneasy quiet that seemed to deepen eerily whenever Felicity turned to the phone and wondered how much longer it would be before she heard from the hospital that Orville was fit enough to be questioned thoroughly.

Felicity sighed. She was beginning to feel very tired and twitchy. She'd had some lunch, thanks to Elaine. She'd even managed to get herself a quick shower in the staff bathroom. It had made her feel better. But so far she hadn't been able to change into a clean shirt. She just didn't have the heart to reclaim the yellow one from Robyn Fisher, who was strutting about in it proudly as part of J.G.'s search party. Almost as proudly as her classmate Benny Stockler, now wearing the duplicate Watchdog name tag that J.G. had given him on being sworn in as a deputy.

And there was still too much to be done for her to go home to change.

The only time she'd been able to relax had been when Mary Farrell had come in and started to fuss with the dummy.

"Just getting him ready for his final rest, Felicity," she'd said solemnly. "Okay?"

Felicity nodded. "Sure, go ahead, Mary!"

It was touching, really, to see how sadly the hard-nosed young window dresser had taken the postponement of the contest. But it was only to be expected, Felicity guessed, from someone who'd put so much of her heart into the original arrangement.

So the "corpse" of Arnold Cripps was laid carefully on the flimsy trestle table that Carl Green and Ernest Snerdoff had borrowed from the Museum Department. It had been almost laughable to hear Mary hiss and insist on "more respect for the deceased" whenever they raised their voices. The driver had groaned despairingly and even Snerdoff had looked guilty.

But Mary had had her way as usual.

So now "Arnold Cripps" was sharing Felicity's vigil while she awaited her vital phone call. His was a remarkably tranquil posture—stretched out full length with his hands folded across his chest. Traces of the layout of the "Farmland Around West Milbury in Colonial Times" were still visible on the table's surface. Somehow Mary had so arranged the body that the dummy's head was outlined by the oxbow curve of the Milbury River—with blue paint for the water and yellow for the build-up of silt.

Another little touch was a small bouquet of flowers that Mary had selected from the vase on the counter and tenderly placed between his folded hands—two or three black-eyed Susans, a bunch of clover, and a haze of baby's breath. The only blemish to the picture of well-earned repose was a huge spider that had scuttled from the dust sheet covering the lower half of the dummy's body. It was now crawling hesitantly across "Arnold's" innocent face.

Felicity groaned softly to think how Orville himself might have ended this way only a couple of hours ago.

That was the end of her relaxation. The investigation had to go on—but *urgently*!

Well, she'd checked the news item about the Charles manuscript. Mr. Peabody had indeed mentioned the possible film deal and even speculated that the news might increase the exhibit's value two- or three-fold.

Also, there was something Elaine had brought to her attention when she came back with the sandwiches.

She must certainly look into *that*!

She dialed the staff lounge.

When she came into the Junior Room, Elaine gave a squeak of alarm at seeing the "body's" new appearance.

"Don't worry about that, Elaine," Felicity said. "It's only for half an hour—until they move it back to the store."

"Mary's idea?"

"Who else's? I'm more interested in what you said about the Kandy Kabin when you brought the sandwiches. . . ."

"Sure, Felicity! What is it you want to know?"

"Something that could possibly nail The Chameleon and get us back the Charles manuscript."

"Wow!" Elaine had always wanted to assist Felicity in her *detective* work as well as her library stuff. "Go ahead!"

"Well, you remember when you stopped off at the Kandy Kabin . . . ?"

"I sure do. I'd just come back from taking Spencer Curtis and his dog home, and on both legs of the journey I'd had to listen to Spencer going on and on about the crunchiness, the munchiness, and the sheer yummy sweetness of his favorite candy."

"Yes, but go on, Elaine. I'm more interested in what the *clerk* said."

"Well, I told you. I *knew* you'd be interested. . . ."

"Yes, I *am*! But his exact words, Elaine?"

Elaine frowned. "Well, I wasn't paying much attention at first. I was too busy breaking into the package I'd just bought. But I certainly pricked up my ears when he said that this was the second time that morning that an adult had been asking for peanut brittle like their life depended on it. Usually it's only kids, he said, and . . ."

"Yes, Elaine. But what was it he said about the man?"

Elaine frowned again. "He . . . he said, 'He works at the library, too.' At least, he said he was doing some job here. . . ."

"Is this what the clerk said to *you*, or what the man said to the clerk?"

"I . . . uh . . . I'm not sure. He . . ."

"Elaine, stop right there!" said Felicity. "This is absolutely vital. I want you to go back immediately and talk to him again. I want as accurate a description of that earlier customer as you can drag out of the guy. A.S.A.P!"

"You bet!" said Elaine. "Can I get you anything while I'm there?"

"No. Just the description. . . ." Elaine's account of Spencer's account of the glorious joys of peanut brittle had set Felicity's mouth watering, too. But time was running out.

While Elaine was gone, Felicity made a couple of extra checks on matters that had started to bother her mind: one, upstairs on the Third Floor, and the other in the Junior Room itself. . . .

24

Detective Delaney Steps In

When Elaine got back half an hour later flushed with triumph, the Junior Room was beginning to look crowded. Besides Felicity Snell, there were Mary Farrell, the driver, Ernest Snerdoff, Mr. Hayes, Gary Vitalis, and Mr. Rubinstein, all looking down at the body. There was also a growing bunch of kids, including J.G., Freddie Fisher, and most of the other Watchdogs.

Everyone appeared suitably awed.

Although bursting with her news, Elaine kept her distance. From what she'd just heard at the Kandy Kabin, she now knew that one of these people was The Chameleon and she didn't want to go anywhere near him.

She also steered clear of Gary Vitalis because she'd heard an ugly rumor that Vitalis was plotting to steal her from the Junior Department and use her in some coffee shop gimmick.

But at least Vitalis wasn't talking about the Internet now.

Mr. Rubinstein probably wouldn't have listened anyway. He seemed far more interested in the "corpse."

"That's a real nice arrangement, Ms. Farrell!" the store owner said. "Tasteful and imaginative as ever."

"Thank you, sir!" said Mary, blushing.

"And it was a masterstroke to cover him with the contest banner! Like laying a soldier to rest draped with the flag."

"That was *his* idea, sir," said Mary, nodding toward the driver and blushing even deeper. She was obviously finding it difficult to make this admission.

Green was smirking now as Mr. Rubinstein said, "It was a good idea, anyway."

"Thank you, sir!" the driver murmured modestly, bending to straighten the dummy's new covering. "It came to me when we brung down the banners ready for returning downtown. It'll sort of give him a more dignified send-off as we take him down to the van. Mr. Snerdoff's been giving me pointers how to do the ceremonial dead march."

Gary Vitalis looked green as he regarded the roughly draped bier. It certainly looked impressive.

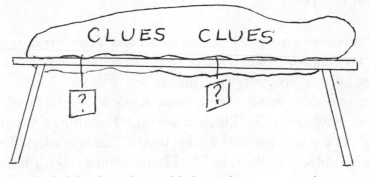

The words did look rather odd, but Elaine guessed Mary would take care of that.

Even as Elaine was thinking this, Mary pushed Green aside and started softening the folds and tucking in the question marks as if preparing a display of bedding.

"Give us ten more minutes, sir." She withdrew the bouquet from under the covers and placed it on top. "Better pin it secure," she said, reaching automatically to her mouth for the pin that wasn't there and swiftly turning to her Scotch tape instead. "Or some klutz is sure to knock it off before it reaches the van!"

"Now this is just the kind of item we could put out on the Internet, sir," said Vitalis as Mr. Rubinstein began to move away.

"Later, Gary," said Mr. Rubinstein. "I'm more interested right now in seeing the impression this makes on the kids outside. And I've got to make sure the news photographers record the fact that Felicity's contest didn't end in *complete* disaster, after all."

"Amen to that!" said Mr. Hayes.

Elaine plucked at Felicity's sleeve. "Felicity!" she hissed. "We've got to talk!"

Felicity nodded. "I guessed as much from your face when you got back from the candy store. I reckon you got a good description, then?"

"Boy! Did I ever!"

But it had taken some coaxing to get *any* description out of the clerk. Like most people, he was totally unreliable when it came to judging heights, weights, ages, and so on.

"But you said he was doing some work at the library," Elaine insisted. "What work? Electric wiring? Plumbing? Gardening? What?" The man kept shaking his head. "Radio repairs? Exterminating? Unblocking drains?" As Elaine went on with her Yellow Pages act, he kept on shrugging and shaking his head until she felt like screaming. "Painting and decorating?" she continued. "TV antenna installation . . . ?"

"Hey, now wait a second. That rings a bell."

"What, TV antenna . . . ?"

"Nargh! Painting and decorating. It did cross my mind he'd been fitting carpets. Yeah . . . That was it!"

"Carpets?" Elaine's head was reeling.

"Yeah. Like we had new ones fitted here only a coupla months ago. After *we'd* painted and decorated. And the carpet fitter—he'd got the same kind of uniform."

"What kind of uniform?"

"Well, just a khaki smock really. With his firm's name on it. Kind of a badge."

"What firm?"

The man touched his chest.

"Rubinstein's. In squiggly red writing. Embroidered right here."

It wasn't much but the clerk couldn't have given a more pinpoint, accurate description if he'd told her the mystery customer's social security number.

"Thanks!" she said.

"Have a nice day," he replied.

"Good work, Elaine!" said Felicity, moving straight to the phone when her aide had reached the end of the report. Most of the others had gone out behind Mr. Snerdoff and Carl Green. The table's legs had been folded up and, as planned, the two men were carrying it like a stretcher, slowly and solemnly.

"Rick?" said Felicity, when someone answered on the first ring. "We've tracked it down!"

Freddie and Ruth looked at each other gleefully. They'd hung behind with Elaine, while J.G. and the others had gone along to witness the effect of the procession on the crowd. Now, the brother and sister were glad that they had. "Rick" was Detective Delaney's nickname.

"No," Felicity was saying. "We don't actually have it in our hands. He's just about to take it away for burial. Yes . . . *burial*. With full military honors. . . . You'll see what I mean when you get here. But make it quick. . . . Yes, at the library. We'll be with him in the parking lot. One of Rubinstein's delivery vans—you can't miss it. We'll stall him if necessary, but we need your official presence for the search and arrest. . . . No, Mary Farrell is completely innocent. . . . She's just been used by him as a cover. You might have to restrain her when she finds out, though. I wouldn't like to be in his shoes *then*! Yes, we certainly do have probable cause. Relax! Just get here!"

If J.G. had been present, he'd have been butting in, urging Delaney to bring a Swat Team. But the young gun-jumper's mood was far from gung ho as he watched the start of the procession.

In fact, it was sad, really. As someone who'd had such high hopes for the contest, J.G. was depressed to think it had come to such an untimely end after Orville's rescue and the theft of the manuscript.

He felt deep regret that Felicity and the Watchdog Squad (that *he* led!) had failed in their search, and he knew the others were feeling that way too: hushed, subdued, disappointed, beat.

Even the sight of Mary's driver stumbling over his first steps in the slow, stiff-legged dead march routine barely raised a titter from the young watchers. Mary looked furious as she supervised the ceremony she'd done so much to arrange.

This was understandable, with Mr. Rubinstein watching every movement and the flashbulbs beginning to pop again.

But she needn't have worried.

By the time they'd gone down the first three steps, Carl Green seemed to have recovered some poise.

Then a lift of the spirits seemed to ripple through the Watchdogs as Felicity caught up, looking her usual bright and energetic self again.

"Come on, you guys," she said. "This isn't a *real* funeral. This is an occasion of great joy!"

"Huh?" J.G. looked as if she could have fooled *him*.

The body was already being lifted by the two men into the back of the van, still on its table/stretcher. Felicity and Elaine climbed in after it, closely followed by Ruth and Julie and Holly, who seemed to have gotten wind that something very special was afoot. Even little Robyn wasn't far behind, fluttering forward in the oversized yellow shirt, looking more like a butterfly than an angel.

"Hey! What *is* this?" rasped Carl Green. "Go back! It's all over now!"

"It will be in another couple of minutes!" said Felicity, spotting a car that was just sliding into the space between the van and the old mobile library.

Felicity's tone had made Mary look up curiously from the piles of books she had selected earlier. Carl Green was now staring at Felicity with alarm as she strode up to the "corpse."

"Hey! Get away from it!" he yelled.

That seemed to be the signal for Ernest Snerdoff to put in his two cents worth. "Don't talk to Ms. Snell like that, pilgrim! I was about to clear this junk off the table myself. It's time it was returned to the Natural History Museum."

"Leave it, I say!" Green almost howled. "I'll take it up myself, later. Soon. When I've just folded up the banners."

"Yes, Mr. Snerdoff," said Felicity. "Give us a minute to pay our last respects to Arnold Cripps . . . and to place this where it belongs."

She was holding out the dummy's name tag.

"Where did you find *that*?" said Mary. "I've been looking all over—"

"No, not *there*!" said Carl Green, snatching the tag from

Felicity's hand as she began to uncover the "corpse." "Where's the dignity in *that*? Here, *here*—next to the flowers on top!"

With a shaking hand, he pinned the tag on the covering banner.

"What's with you, Carl Green?" said Mary. "Trying to steal my job as a window display technician?" She turned. "Anyway, where *did* you find the tag, Felicity?"

"Up in the janitor's storeroom. This afternoon."

"Huh?" grunted Ernest Snerdoff. "*I* didn't put it there, Ms. Snell!"

"I know you didn't, Mr. Snerdoff. *He* did!"

There was no sound from Carl Green now except for a faint strangled choking noise.

But that may have been because Detective Rick Delaney had just entered the van looking very stern.

25

The Last Laugh

"Okay, Felicity," said the detective, "where is it, this twenty-five-thousand-dollar manuscript?"

"Right here!" said Felicity.

Carefully, she removed the flowers and unpinned the name tag. Then she whipped off the cover itself, setting the question mark cards flying in all directions.

There was dead silence. All they could see at first was the same dumb dummy lying full length with its hands folded on its chest as Mary had left it. The spider, which had seemed to be whispering into the dummy's ear, scuttled away.

It was an eerie moment. Also a very tense one for Felicity, with no stolen manuscript to be seen and a busy police detective impatient to view it.

The smirking glint had started to creep back into Green's eyes.

Then Felicity grabbed the dummy and flung it over onto its front.

There was a gasp of relief from the surrounding Watchdogs.

The strange, long, leather-bound volume was staring up at them all. Its fine gold lettering winked at them in the beam of the flashlight Delaney was shining on it. It read, *The Serial Version of THE CORSICAN CONSPIRACY by HENRY CHARLES*.

"I guess it gives a whole new meaning to your description of the perp as a 'Serial Sneak Thief,' Felicity!" said Detective Delaney, grinning.

"Huh!" grunted the perp, not grinning.

Felicity, too, ignored the joke. "He must have thrust it there quickly when he brought it down with the folded banners. From whatever temporary hiding place he'd stashed it in. Probably the janitor's storeroom."

"Is that correct?" said the detective to the scowling Green, who now muttered something about the Fifth Amendment.

"We'll see about that!" said Delaney, turning back to Felicity. She was now holding up the Arnold Cripps name tag, again.

"Does that have anything to do with the case?"

"Yes!" said Felicity. "I have every reason to believe Mr. Green used it to lure the boy, Orville Grisson, to the roof."

"The kid who was rescued . . . ?" began Delaney.

"Yes, by Felicity!" said Ruth Fisher, fiercely. "And she nearly got herself killed doing it!"

"Yeah!" growled Robyn, clinging onto Felicity's leg as if to save her from a fifty-foot drop.

"Reckless endangerment!" said J.G., getting out his pipe for this one. "Aren't you going to book him for that, as well?"

"All in good time," said Delaney.

"And he's got something in his pocket, right now," said J.G. "Something long and tubular wrapped in greaseproof paper. Just poking out." He was giving it the full hard scrutiny of his steely right eye. "It could be a gun barrel. Or . . . or a blowpipe for poison darts. Isn't it about time you frisked him?"

"Yes!" said Holly Jenks. "We could all be killed!"

Delaney sighed. "I'm afraid I *will* have to search you, sir."

Green shrugged, giving J.G. and Holly a very dirty look. "Be my guest, officer. The boy's nuts. It runs in his family. I know."

"Watch it, klutz!" growled Mary.

"Hardly lethal," said the detective, removing the tight roll of paper and beginning to unroll it. Then his grin faded as he stared at the rows of labels stuck to it, ready to be unpeeled and stuck some-place else. Just *where*, he couldn't imagine!

But the others could, as they too stared at the rows of laughter—all in the same style of printing but in several different sizes, ready to be stuck to clue cards as the driver pretended to help Mary select her books.

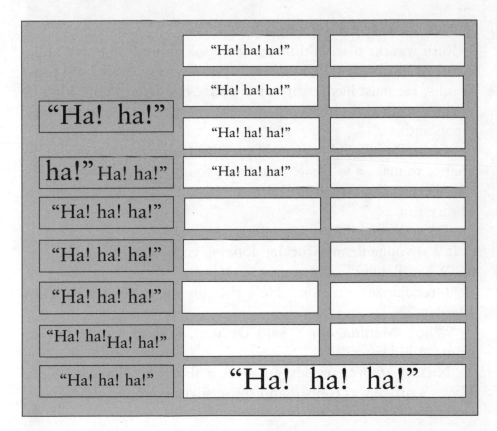

"And it has direct bearing on the theft of the manuscript," said Felicity. "Would you ask Ms. Fitch to come down right away, Holly? Tell her it's to identify the stolen manuscript. And to tell the detective where *this* had been left."

She brought out the defaced information card The Chameleon had left behind.

Detective Delaney seemed to make up his mind as he saw the printed laughter that had been stuck across the manuscript's typed description.

"That's a match in *my* book. Looks like the last laugh's on you, sir."

This opened up the floodgates.

Ruth was the first. "I'd throw the book at him!" she said indignantly. "The book called *Oliver Twist. That's* where he got those laughs. He must have torn out the pages to get at them. I bet he cut them out and photocopied them and glued them onto these labels and . . ."

"Okay, Ruth," said Felicity. "Detective Delaney will give you the chance to make a full statement later. You may even show him the very book." She turned to Delaney. "It's only next door in the old library van. . . ."

"Do you mind if *I* say something, ma'am?"

It was young Benny Stockler, looking very excited.

"What, Benny?"

"I recognize him now! He's the guy that messed with my Matilda."

"Who's Matilda, son?" said Delaney, looking suddenly very grim. "A kid sister?"

"No. My *ferret*, sir. He got her to slip her collar when Mr. Hayes's office was robbed and those silver cups and things were stolen."

"Hey, yes!" growled Ernest Snerdoff. "Including my award for the Best Kept Library Lobby in the Northeast. *Whadidja do with it, jerk?*" He rounded on Green with such a furious glare and a flexing of tattooed forearm muscles that Delaney had to step in.

But not before Spencer had chipped in with *his* beef.

"If you searched those pockets with a vacuum thing, sir, I bet you'd find chips and slivers and bits of the peanut brittle that he tried to bait my dog with. And I bet Sweets would soon sniff 'em out if we brung him back now, Elaine."

"Some other time, Spence," said Elaine. "I don't think my diet program would stand up to it twice in one day!"

"Come on!" said Delaney to the flinching shadow of what was once the master criminal that had terrorized the Ebenezer Twitch-purse Memorial Library. "We're going downtown."

"Gladly!" said the villain, offering up his wrists for cuffing. "Before these nuts decide to take the law into their own hands!"

26

Felicity Discovers the Truth

Carl Green lived alone in a trailer in a clearing in some woods several miles out of town. When the police searched it later, it didn't take them long to find the trophies that had been stolen from Mr. Hayes's office all those months ago. They were dirty and in pretty poor shape, but they were all there. It was obvious from the state they were in that he hadn't been planning to sell them. When pressed by Delaney, he admitted he'd been using them for target practice. They'd been pocked and scarred by shotgun pellets. And wherever the name Ebenezer Twitchpurse Memorial had been engraved, attempts had been made to scratch it out—deeply, angrily, savagely, by the look of it.

But he wouldn't say why, at first.

Money obviously hadn't been the motive for stealing these things.

This was borne out by the fact that the TV star's twenty-thousand-dollar coat was still on the premises. They found it stuffed in a broken outhouse window to keep the rain out.

"Have you any idea how valuable this *was*?" Delaney asked him.

"Sure," was the reply. "Isn't that the way valuable things always get treated at that place?"

The detective thought it proved the guy was nuts, but Felicity wasn't so sure.

"It seems to me that Professor Ames was right," she said.

"Who's he?"

"The profiler who figured The Chameleon had a grudge against the library."

"Oh yeah? But why? Fined too much for an overdue book?"

"No," said Felicity. "But I bet a book has *something* to do with it."

She spent the next couple of days digging into the library's archives down in the basement, going through old diaries and back numbers of the *West Milbury Gazette*. It was tedious, dirty work and she turned down various offers of help from Watchdogs and others.

"You wouldn't know what to look for," she said. "Even I don't—until I see it."

"That's what detective work's really all about," said J.G. to the others, sadly, wisely, as if he'd spent half his life combing through dumps himself. "Can't Mr. Delaney *scare* the truth out of him?"

"No!" said Felicity, returning to the basement yet again.

And, in the end, she did find what she was looking for.

Not the book itself. But mention of it in one labeled *Minutes of the E.T.M. Library Reference Department Local Collection Committee*. In an entry dated September 13, 1982, there was a list headed: *Books offered but rejected*. And first on that list was *The Green Anole or American Chameleon: A Study* by Carl Bradley Green, The Willow Bend Press.

"*Him*? *Our* Chameleon? Mary's driver?" gasped J.G. when he heard the news.

"No, his father," said Felicity, sounding rather sad despite her discovery. "He had taught biology locally. I vaguely remember him myself. Now that I have the book's title, I've been able to follow up. It seems he spent years writing it only to have it rejected by publisher after publisher. Finally, he *paid* to have it published privately. He presented a copy to this library. Ms. Fitch turned it down and who can blame her? She'd found out that whole chunks of the book had been copied from studies already published."

Felicity broke this news at a Mystery Club meeting in the old library van.

"It seems to be a habit with that family," said Ruth. "Stealing from other people's books." She was eyeing the plundered volume of *Oliver Twist*.

"Yes," said Felicity. "But it isn't a capital offense. . . ."

She sounded so sad that Ruth looked up sharply. "You mean . . . ?"

"I'm afraid that Carl Green Senior shot himself soon after this in 1982. When his son was only twelve."

"So *that* was the motive," said J.G. "Revenge!"

"I'm sure the judge will take it into account," said Felicity. "When he gets these facts. Meanwhile, cheer up, everyone. The Cluefinders Contest is going to be completed this coming Saturday."

And it was.

With Benny the winner and Orville Grisson a close second.

In fact, it should have been a tie but Orville very graciously conceded the victory to Benny. "I mean, it was the kid who found Clue Number One first," he said.

This did nothing to take away from Orville's newfound popularity.

After all, it wasn't every kid who got to go to police headquarters and pick out a suspected felon from a lineup. Especially when it was the guy who'd endangered the kid's life up on the library roof.

J.G. had instantly adopted Orville as a partner for that alone.

As for Mary Farrell, she'd been furious at having been used as an accomplice by The Chameleon, and even more so by having her brother rubbing it in for days afterward. But she soon got over it when she heard that the publicity about the dummy's "funeral" display had attracted attention in New York, and with it, the offer of a special window display training course at the university.

As Mr. Rubinstein told her, "If we're not careful, we'll be losing you to Macy's, young lady!"

Even Arnold Cripps seemed to have a smile on his face in the store's main window, now that he was fully dressed in a fine Italian designer suit and the expensive raincoat that Mary had so furiously rejected that first morning.

The only reward that didn't bring a smile to the face of the recipients at first was the one for Sweets and Spencer. It was a special obedience and dog-handling course supervised by Felicity herself.

Its main feature was a strict diet as far as sugary snacks were concerned, with only one half-bite-size piece of peanut brittle allowed on any one day.

"I guess he'll learn to live with it," said Spencer.

"I'm sure you both will," said Felicity cheerfully. "The same diet goes for you, too! But you'll thank me for it in the end."